Readers love
MIA KERICK

Here Without You

"Like the first book, there are some wonderful, positive messages interwoven into the narrative about hope for the future, healthy and loving relationships, and communication."

—It's About The Book

"I absolutely loved the way Mia Kerick handled their growing relationship intimacy."

—The Kimi-chan Experience

Random Acts

"I definitely recommend this book to other fans of m/m romance, and I look forward to reading more by this author."

—Rainbow Gold Reviews

"…I was swept away in the grandiose romance between Brad and Caleb, two men who are fundamentally different but fit together like puzzle pieces."

—My Fiction Nook

Out of Hiding

"*Out of Hiding* by Mia Kerick is simply outstanding, and I highly recommend this novel to you."

—The Novel Approach

"Overall, this was a really good story about figuring out who you are, what you want, and that life is all about taking risks to achieve true happiness."

—MM Good Book Reviews

By MIA KERICK

Beggars and Choosers • Unfinished Business
Grand Adventures (Dreamspinner Anthology)
It Could Happen
Out of Hiding
A Package Deal
Random Acts

ONE VOICE
Published by Harmony Ink Press: Us Three
Here Without You

Published with Harmony Ink Press
Intervention
Not Broken, Just Bent
The Red Sheet

Published by DREAMSPINNER PRESS
www.dreamspinnerpress.com

IT COULD HAPPEN

MIA KERICK

Published by
DREAMSPINNER PRESS

5032 Capital Circle SW, Suite 2, PMB# 279, Tallahassee, FL 32305-7886 USA
www.dreamspinnerpress.com

It Could Happen
© 2017 Mia Kerick.

Cover Art
© 2017 Aaron Anderson.
aaronbydesign55@gmail.com
Cover content is for illustrative purposes only and any person depicted on the cover is a model.

ISBN: 978-1-63533-688-7
Digital ISBN: 978-1-63533-689-4
Library of Congress Control Number: 2017902895
Published June 2017
v. 1.0

Printed in the United States of America
∞
This paper meets the requirements of
ANSI/NISO Z39.48-1992 (Permanence of Paper).

To love triangles everywhere

CHAPTER 1
MEET THE PLAYERS

Brody's notebook

MONDAY, SEPTEMBER 15

Before I bare my soul on paper, I'd like to set the record straight.
1. I'm not a ten-year-old girl.
2. My journal isn't pink and fuzzy with a heart-shaped lock.
3. I don't make daily entries with a magenta gel pen.
4. There's nothing simple about bromance.
I feel better after getting that off my chest—my flat chest, and I'm not in the market for a training bra. See #1, above.

My end goal is to create a user manual for my relationship with Henry and Danny, because I'm seriously confused about where we go from here—wherever *here* is—and how we get past everything that stands in our way to make it there. In theory, if I write down what goes on with us, I'll be able to read it back to myself and make sense of things before I do something stupid and/or dangerous.

To get back to my original point, I am *not* keeping a diary. It's just the third section of my AP Physics notebook, which I consider a safe place to record my most top-secret thoughts about life, as nobody on earth gives a shit about my half-assed notes.

Maybe I'm *not* the creative one, but I can write stuff down as well as the next guy. And everybody knows that getting started is the hardest part, so I won't obsess over it... too much.

I'll start here, about Henry.

Mostly Henry Perkins strives to live life by the book—it makes it easier to deal with his parents' rules and expectations. The problem is that the smaller, more insistent—and much hornier—part of Henry wants to do whatever the hell he wants to do. But the thing is, Henry can't get any of the stuff he wants if he lives by the book, which his mom and dad wrote.

I nailed that summary, so I'll move on to Danny.

Next there's Danny Denisco, who *is* the creative one. He can do stuff like write poetry and paint pictures and still not come off as lame. I can sum up what he wants in a couple of simple sentences. Danny wants only one thing out of life and, more specifically, from the guys he goes out with. And no, it's not sex. Danny's looking for the L word, but *his* problem is that he'll settle for any liar's promise of affection, and lie is the *wrong* L word.

Then there's me. It's tough to look objectively at the big picture of yourself, conclude that "Brody Decker's main objective is to _____," and then fill in the blank with something profound. Because all kinds of shit comes to mind when I think about what *I* want—to feel the wind in my face and to find the highest adrenaline rush of all time are on the top of the list. But there's this other guy in me. He gets freaked out easily, so he lives life by the "don't ask, don't tell" code. I'm starting to think he wants some of the stuff Henry and Danny want too.

Wind and adrenaline don't take much effort to find where there's speed, and I've got that part covered. But maybe I want the stuff Henry and Danny want *more*.

Henry: My life

BRODY'S NOT even a member of the Thomas Bailey Aldrich High School Cross-Country Team, but he's always the first one to get to practice. The dude can run—he's the fastest runner *not* on the team. And he has more endurance than even *I* have, and that's saying something, since he's vegan. Over the years, whenever I suggest he officially join the team, Brody refuses. "I'm not the *joiner* type," he said again, just yesterday. Honestly I give up. Brody wouldn't listen to reason if his life depended on it, which it sometimes does.

When I get to the field today he's in his usual spot behind the dugout, simultaneously fastening a bandana around his spiky bleach-blond hair, doing walking lunges to stretch his quads and hamstrings, and chatting it up with Coach.

"Hey, Henry, you're late. Coach and I wondered if you were going to grace us with your presence today," he quips.

And Coach Wentworth appreciates his humor. He smiles and says, "Yeah, Perkins. Drop and give me one hundred sit-ups, ten for every minute you were late."

"But I had to talk to Mr. Duke about a European Civ quiz I messed up on." I let go of my gym bag and squat down to change my sneakers. Coach mumbles something like "stop whining," so I hit the ground and pay the price for being late.

Brody flops down on the grass at my side and does sideways sit-ups in time with mine. "Did he make you beg?" he asks.

"Did *who* do *what*?" I'm short with him because he's responsible for the burn in my belly.

"Duke—did you have to kiss his ass so he'd let you retake the quiz?"

"Basically, yeah," I grunt.

"Duke's the king of assholes." Brody chuckles. "Did you catch that? I put two kinds of royalty in one short sentence."

I shake my head because Brody's mind wanders a lot, even while churning out sit-ups. "My folks won't let me go to the corn maze next weekend if Mr. Duke calls home about a bad quiz grade."

Brody stops doing sit-ups and stares at me. "I'll help you study, Henry, because you and Danny and me, we're going to the dang corn maze next Saturday night, and then you guys are sleeping at my house. We planned it eons ago."

As soon as I finish the hundredth sit-up, I open my legs and bend forward to stretch out my calves. "We *tentatively* planned it."

I always need to correct Brody on stuff like that, seeing as he tends to forget shit he doesn't *want* to remember. "Mom and Dad haven't technically given me the all clear on the sleepover yet but—"

"You *said* we were going to have a sleepover. *You said*," Brody whines and then jumps to his feet, sprints across the field, and does some kind of a crazy backflip in the air. The whole cross-country team gawks at him, and then they look at me, 'cause I'm known as Brody Decker's keeper.

"Control your boy." The remark comes from number two on the team, Lionel Wagner. He'd love to see me and Brody long gone. He hates competition when he's not the guy set to win.

"I'm on it," I say to nobody in particular. "Decker. Get over here and stretch with me so you don't get cramps in your calves when you're whoopin' Wagner's ass out there on the trail!"

LIKE ALWAYS we're the first two to hit the road, and the rest of the team follows behind. Lionel always makes a point to be the last to leave the field so it isn't obvious how much faster I am. Brody's faster than him too, even if he's not officially a Golden Eagle, a fact that stomps on Wagner's overgrown ego. But Brody lingers behind.

"Let's go, dude."

"You said I could whoop his ass," he argues. "So I need to hang back."

I counter, "Nah, run with me instead." I'm team captain, and even if Brody's just there for the hell of it, he has to do what I say. And I'm selfish. "You're running with me."

We talk and jog for the first mile, knowing we'll get down to the serious business of running for the next four miles. Truthfully the talking part is more of a challenge for me than the running part, but I do it because he's Brody. He sucks at discussing serious shit, but he's good at small talk and talking Danny and me down off ledges.

"So you're sending in the early admission application to Prospect University, right?" Brody asks as we start down School Street.

4

I expect that question. "I wrote the essay and filled out most of the online forms, if that's what you're asking."

"Have you requested your recommendations yet?"

"I'm... working... on... it." The way I say it—slow and cautious—makes me sound reluctant. But I don't *feel* reluctant. I just feel worried. One of my teachers might mention something about it to my parents at church or a cross-country meet.

"And remember, you can use my credit card so your parents don't find out you're applying," Brody said. "My parents won't care. They don't even look at my credit card statement before they write the check."

We all know that my dad won't like it if I so much as *consider* a school that isn't Division 1 in men's track. But since Prospect University is D2, I can still get a big enough scholarship to make it totally doable, if not as glamorous. Dad hasn't yet figured out that I'm eighteen years old and can do what I want, and *I* haven't figured out how to inform him.

"Has Danny been working on *his* application?" I ask. That part is critical.

"He says he's got everything finished but insists he's not going to get accepted to Prospect because his grades suck."

"They're gonna see his paintings, right?" I need to be reassured that Danny stands a chance of getting in, because Prospect University is our only chance of sticking together after high school. The academic requirements aren't too tough, so Danny and Brody will most likely get accepted, and there's the big and necessary scholarship possibility for me. If it isn't all three of us, the plan is null and void. I'll be off to a NCAA Division I Christian college, Danny will get a job at Walmart or some other place where they won't give him enough hours to get benefits, and Brody will be God-knows-where, chasing storms.

"Yeah. He emailed his portfolio to them."

"Cool. Then he's gonna get accepted." Danny's art is amazing, if not a little bit unusual. Once they see it, Prospect U will want him.

5

Feeling lighter I pick up speed and say, "Stop being such a lardass, Decker. You're holding me back."

Brody is the one who specializes in dishing out humorous harassment. But he has a hard time taking it, even from me. "Get your dang recommendations, Perky," he yells as he sprints past.

Brody's notebook

WEDNESDAY, SEPTEMBER 17
I've decided that this journal needs a title for maximum impact on future readers. And choosing a title is serious business. It's like making a commitment to tone and style.
~~Are You There God? It's Me, Brody~~
So this happened today:
Lionel Wagner again proved that he has mastered the art of being an asshole. His mommy would be so proud.

"FOR THE record, *Danielle*, which do you like better—white meat or dark?" That was how he started.

You can find the Jocks"R"Us lunch table right next to the "Island of Misfit Toys" table, and, in my opinion, it's no coincidence. Although the close proximity provides the jocks ease of messing with our heads, there *is* a bright side. Lionel doesn't have to shout his slander—usually directed at Danny, a.k.a. Danielle—across a cafeteria packed full of students with big ears and bigger mouths. *Yay.*

"I'm putting my money on the dark." That little gem came from the lips of "No-neck" Ned Nelson. Not all the jocks are assholes, but at Thomas Bailey Aldrich High School, those who are don't hold back.

Wagner's smirk nearly pushed me over the edge, but his friends were entertained, which was the whole point. Three of them hooted, four of them literally howled, and they all exchanged high fives, which brought to mind the mating call of the North American Grouse. I can thank Mom and Dad for my extensive knowledge of bird calls—since they retired they've become big fans of the National Geographic Channel, and we have a television in virtually every room of our house.

I was just about to inform Lionel Wagner that he's the perfect image of an asshole—not that I've ever closely examined one—when Henry got up from our table and stalked over to Lionel, looking like he wanted to kick ass and take names. He stuck a finger in Lionel's face and asked, "You got a fuckin' problem, Wagner? I mean, other than the obvious...."

Have you ever cheered silently inside your head at the same time you mumbled, "Oh shit," aloud in a crowded cafeteria? Well, I did today.

When Lionel stood up, I knew that all hell was likely to break loose. "What's *that* supposed to mean?"

"What do you *think* it means?" Henry asked, on his game.

Seeing as poultry was not on the day's hot-lunch menu, I was confident the question Lionel asked, which had started the whole confrontation, clearly pertained to Danny Denisco's preferences regarding an entirely *different* sort of meat. Henry and Lionel—and everybody else within spitting distance—knew that someone had to step up and protect Danny's honor or he was going to take matters into his own hands, which is not a pretty sight. Normally we tag team on shit like that, but seeing as Henry was already on his feet, it fell to him, or as Lionel suggested, "dark meat."

And at that point, Henry's eyes lit up in a bad way. Not that there's a good way for eyes to pop out of someone's head.

Here's a little background info, in the event somebody finds this notebook in a box buried in the attic in a hundred years, when I'm nothing more than dust and a bad memory. Thomas Bailey Aldrich High School is not a playground of diversity in terms of sexuality, gender identity, *or* ethnicity. In addition to Danny, the school's only out gay kid, there are zero transgender students—or at least none willing to reveal it to our vicious student body. Exactly five African American kids, three Asian girls who happen to be sisters, and one dark-skinned guy who refuses to pay the cash to Ancestry.com so he can account for his ethnic origins are the only minorities that attend our "straight as an arrow," white-bread high school.

And yes, I'm aware I mixed metaphors, but *hello*, as Danny would say—it's *my* notebook, and I'll do as I please. *So sue me!* Danny would also say that.

The two black seniors are Henry and Lionel. They find themselves thrown together all the time because they're both strong students and above-average athletes, but everybody knows that they're compared because Henry and Lionel are the only black guys in the senior class. They're also fierce competitors. But they don't hit it off because Henry is cool, and Lionel, as I mentioned before, is a complete and total asshole.

Jamie Carson, a basketball player who attends the Perkins family's holy-roller church and sits at Lionel's "all the jocks in lunch block B except Henry Perkins" lunch table, stepped up and pushed them apart. "You guys have a meet today. Do you really want to get suspended for fighting?"

Henry retreated with the parting words, "Lay off Denisco. You got that, Wagner?" I was certain that Perky's mind had wandered to the potential ugly confrontation he would have with his parents were he forced to explain a suspension during cross-country season.

Lionel muttered loud enough for everybody to hear, "Yup. Danielle's gonna be sucking down dark meat tonight," which made the jocks snicker. All in all Wagner got what he wanted. He got under Henry's skin before an important cross-country meet, increasing his own chances at individual victory. Harassing the school's token gay kid was just a bonus.

Whatever happened to "there's no I in team"?

Here's the confidential shit I won't say to Henry's face.

I don't know many jocks who like to be accused of being light in their cross-trainers, and Henry's no exception. But I'm no jock, and my parents are completely out of touch. They couldn't give a shit if I came out as gay or if I got suspended, or if I did both center stage in the TBA High School auditorium while wearing a clown suit, so I don't much care what the wrathful peanut gallery thinks of me. They can't touch me, and they know it.

I should have been the one to speak up in the caf today.

After the near confrontation, Henry returned to the table, somehow looking both pissed off and guilty. "Those assholes had better not fuck with him again," he said to me across the table.

Which naturally pissed Danny off. "Um… hello!" He shouted like he usually does when we talk about him right in front of his face, and he waved at Henry from his seat beside me. "I'm right here and—news flash—I have ears. They work too. So, don't pretend like I can't hear what you're saying." He made claws with his dark purple fingernails, growled, and then finished telling Henry off with, "If you'd give me a chance, I could take care of that ass-wipe all by my lonesome."

Danny can be intimidating. I've seen him put a kid in his place with just the use of his sharp tongue, but sharp fingernails provide an added deterrent.

Still, times like this make me wish I were 6'3" and made of muscle, like Henry. I'd take Lionel Wagner down, suspension or not. Then I'd take down all the jerk-offs at that testosterone-loaded lunch table, because if those guys aren't asking Danny whether he prefers his "meat" white or dark, they're asking him what it's like to be the filling in a Henry-Brody sandwich cookie—which hits a little too close to home because it sounds so dang sweet—or if he's going to a funeral, seeing as all his clothes are black. And since Danny dates older guys from outside the school, everybody thinks he's somebody's boy toy.

But it's not like that. Danny's sweet in a "rough around the edges" way. Seems only Henry and I are aware of that.

It was so satisfying when Mother Nature shut them all up. I couldn't have planned it any better myself. In the courtyard behind the cafeteria, the wind snapped a long branch off the shade tree. Most of the kids in the cafeteria screamed when it crashed into the window. Even the tough guys dropped their spoons onto their lunch trays.

I just smiled, but even now, lying on my bed and writing in my notebook, I get goose bumps on my arms when I think of the collective shock and awe.

Free verse poetry by Danny D

"Sand"
specks too tiny to see just one
but bound together by the wind
it can
chafe the skin from my face,
crunch like rocks between my teeth,
form pebbles in the corners of my watering eyes,
invade my nose and sting my ears….
it cannot
be missed….
we are like sand in wind

Brody's notebook

FRIDAY, SEPTEMBER 19
~~The Bromance Bible~~ *Um… no.*

Today was epic. I never want to forget it.
Here's what happened:
Henry started to yell before my Jeep even came to a full stop on the street in front of Danny's building. "Hurry up, Danny—get your ass in!"

Henry's not a guy to yell. In fact he doesn't say too much at all. But he's usually pretty direct with Danny and me. I figure he has to bend and stretch the truth so much when he talks to his parents that he completely lets go in our company.

I take a different approach when dealing with my friends, mostly because I like to bust on them. It keeps things light.

So when it was my turn, I went with, "What are you staring at, Danny? Haven't you ever seen two hot guys in a lime-green Jeep Wrangler before?" I rolled my hips and winked, knowing it would get a rise out of him. Danny wrinkled his nose and flipped me the bird, as though my teasing pissed him off, but I know he loved it.

"You said hot guys, Brody?" Danny looked all around the Jeep and then asked me, "Well, where the hell are they?"

For the record, Danny will dish out shit to pretty much anybody, but he'll take it lying down only from Henry and me. His usual response to harassment is shriveling the offender's soul with a look to kill. He's also been known to scratch when pushed too far—and he has seven suspensions to prove it.

Staying true to his nonconformist soul, Danny didn't step in the direction of the Jeep, as instructed. Instead he remained glued to the sidewalk and looked bored. And as always Danny was an eyeful. The first of the fall leaves blew around his knobby knees, which were easy to see in his skintight black jeans. And with a sudden gust, his black-velvet *tunic*—Danny's word—blew up high enough to give us a nice view of his pale, boney chest. Even then Danny didn't make a move toward the Jeep. All he did was fold his arms across his chest to sort of control the parachuting of his... his tunic.

"Any time now, Danny...." Henry was more impatient than usual. "Today's away cross-country meet was cancelled, and my parents don't have a clue. I think I might be free until seven o'clock tonight."

"Henry, you are *so* by the book." Danny shook his head, but he took a step toward the Jeep.

"That's because his parents wrote the book," I added, trying not to laugh.

"Where are we going? 'Cause I've got to be home at seven too. This guy I'm into at the restaurant is gonna come by when he gets off work." When Danny said that, he wouldn't look at us.

When it comes to shit like that, Henry's never too subtle. He said something like "Better not be that thug fry cook, Jared," but he still leaned over and grabbed Danny's hand.

"What if it *is* Jared?" Danny asked as he teetered on the Jeep's side step like he hadn't yet decided if he was going to come along.

"Just get your ass in" were Henry's exact words as he climbed from the passenger seat into the backseat.

Moments of freedom are few and far between in Henry's life. Danny and I are aware of that. So when Danny said, "Okay, I'm in," I knew we were on the same page.

Danny climbed up, dropped into the passenger seat, and buckled. I never start driving until I hear two seat belts click.

I drive too fast. Henry and Danny don't like it, but they don't get on my case unless I'm completely out of control. When I'm going eighty in the Jeep with the top down and the sides off, and wind is whipping through my hair, there's only one word for how I feel—Alive.

As I sped along, the wind blew patterns in Danny's silky dark hair and made it stick out in every direction, but it also smoothed out the angry lines on his face. I glanced back at Henry. I already knew his curls wouldn't be blowing around because he wears them tight to his head, but his eyes were squeezed shut like he was fighting the wind. I think he would have been better off if he just let the wind do its job and blow away all the worries about cross-country times, stellar grades, and religious-fanatic parents who want to control his every move. But nobody asked me.

That was when Danny yelled at me across the center console, "Where are we going?"

I refused to tell him the specifics because I knew he'd try to change my mind. "Into the wind," I yelled back, and when I burst into laughter, a glob of spit escaped the corner of my mouth.

I hope like hell it didn't fly back and hit Henry in the face.

And so we headed east out of Cullfield, toward the coast.

IT COULD HAPPEN

WHEN WE got to Branton Beach, I could hardly hear Henry's voice over the roar of the wind. He shouted something along the line of, "Shit, dude. The wind's fuckin' fierce here. You sure it's safe? Shit, dude." And then a crushed-up paper bag blew past my nose, but it was gone before I could bat it away. The wind was seriously out of control. It was so cool.

"Don't worry. Winifred's been downgraded to a tropical storm," I yelled back. It was fact, but Henry still looked worried.

We parked in the Branton Beach public lot, in the spot closest to the water. When I first pulled into the parking space, Henry protested because it had one of those blue handicapped signs cemented into the sidewalk in front of it, but I reasoned with him and said, "Look around, Perky. Nobody but us is at the beach today, so stop being such a Boy Scout and shut up."

By that point all three of us had managed to crowd together in the front seat of the Jeep. Danny's the smallest, so he had to straddle the console. One heavy black boot was pressed onto my thigh, the other on Henry's. We all squinted as we studied the waves in the distance, because the sand stung our eyes.

Danny covered his face with his hands and made a comment like "The sand is exfoliating my skin."

The way I see it, Danny doesn't need that kind of beauty treatment. The kid's like a male, Goth Snow White with his pale skin and dark hair and red lips. The way he looked right then—all pink-cheeked and pretty—*almost* distracted me. And whenever I don't want to deal with how I feel, I change things up. So I shouted, "Let's go down to the water and check out the waves." I grabbed my camera, and we all got out of the Jeep.

I couldn't stop myself from running to the boardwalk. Like always Henry and Danny lingered behind. Once I was on the white sandy beach, I stopped, lifted my face to the sky, and took it all in. The clouds were a threatening gray, but it was dry, and the air seemed strangely warm. And even though the tide wasn't high, it wasn't disappointing. I got to see the best wave display *ever* at Branton Beach. Each huge wave rolled over the one before it, and the white water at the peaks must have reached twenty feet from the ocean's surface. There was mist where the waves crashed together. I could taste the salt in the air. Sand stung my eyes, stuck in between my teeth, and filled my ears.

I remember thinking it was better than sex. Not that I had any way of knowing that.

Henry came up from behind me. "Shit! Like, holy shit!"

"Epic," I corrected him, but since I didn't yell, my word blew away in the wind.

We took a few steps back and grabbed Danny's skinny wrists to pull him up between us. Then we stood close together in a line, as though three boys could form a wall against Winifred's fury. Between the wind and the sand and the waves and my friends, my senses were full.

But the full feeling only lasted a few seconds.

A tug in my heart I didn't want to feel pulled me away from my wall of friends. I sprinted toward the water. As I ran toward the crashing waves, I lifted the camera to my face and snapped the most amazing shots since the ones I took during the thunderstorm on Pierce Hill in July, when I felt certain I was going to be zapped by a bolt of lightning.

At that point I was on autopilot. I kicked off my hiking boots, which I always wear untied, and yanked my T-shirt over my head. Then I wrapped up my camera in my shirt and ran down to the water.

That's not exactly the full story. It really went more like this:

I could hear Danny and Henry shouting my name, but I tuned them out and tuned Mother Nature in. I ran straight into the water and got knocked right down. A wave—the Hulk Hogan of waves—pushed and pulled me like a ragdoll. I should have been scared, but I wasn't. Not at all.

I was energized because I was part of Nature's fury. I didn't have to think or feel or worry anymore. When I finally managed to stand up, my heart pounded as though I'd run a 5K. My adrenaline spiked to legendary levels, and my lungs screamed for oxygen. My brain kept asking, "What comes next?" But then I felt big hands on the back of my shorts. They pulled me away from the wildness and the exhilaration.

Oh… and the danger.

Once we were on the dry sand, Henry yelled into my ear, "What the fuck are you thinking, dude?"

I stuttered something like, "I'm just… it's just…." I had no idea how to explain what I was thinking when I decided it would be a good idea to take a swim in the churning ocean. I decided to go with distraction instead of a lame explanation, so I said, "Let's lie on top of the snack hut, huh? We can climb up there and be one with the wind."

This is a major reason why I love Henry. He almost never lectures me about how I take unnecessary risks with my life, because he knows me. And he knows that the chances I take are very necessary. Without them I'd probably shrivel up and blow away like that paper bag in the wind.

He just said, "Cool. Go get your shirt and camera and boots, and I'll grab Danny."

Within five minutes Henry knelt on top of the Branton Beach Snack Shack's metal roof and pulled up Danny, who kept on calling me "a major dipshit." I helped out by pushing up on his biker boots. Once he was on the roof, I grabbed on to both Henry and Danny's dangling hands, and they hoisted me up. Then we lay flat on our backs in a tight row on top of the gritty metal roof—Henry and Danny on either side of me—so close I could feel the sand on their arms grinding against the sand on mine. And once my heart stopped pounding, I grabbed Danny's small hand and Henry's big one. They squeezed my palms enough to hurt—both of them—but I knew I deserved the pain. It was fair punishment and so much better than a lecture.

"Dipshit—you're a dipshit!" Danny yelled the word into the sky. He must have been mad at me too, because his voice was louder than the roar of the waves and wind combined.

After about the tenth time, I shouted back, "Maybe so, but I'm *your* dipshit." And I squeezed their hands, but not too hard.

It was epic.

CHAPTER 2
ONE MAN DOWN

Free verse poetry by Danny D

I was *not* okay
being alone.
So how can it be that I am even less okay
being with him?
~my face is his punching bag
~sex is just sex
~he tells me how I should feel
Do I need another reason to say goodbye?
Yet I cling to him, so afraid to lose my grip
On the one I belong to…
Today.
I will be chained in someone else's backyard tomorrow.

Henry: My life

SOMETHING'S OFF with Danny. He didn't come to the movies with us on Saturday night because he had a date with that thirty-five-year-old fry cook he met at work. I spent this Sunday, like all the rest, with my family, doing the church and Sunday-dinner thing, but Brody texted me that night to let me know that Danny never returned his calls. And Danny was out of school yesterday.

When we stopped by his apartment after cross-country practice today, he didn't answer the door. Maybe he wasn't home, but Brody's got "inner feelings" about things, and he says Danny was in there. I tend to believe him.

You can't distract Brody when he's worried about one of us, although he *uses* distraction to throw us off track when we're worried about him. And since we're almost *always* worried about him, he has to distract us *a lot*.

"I just want to hear Danny say he's okay. Until I hear that, I'm not going to stop trying to reach him." Brody's draped across my bed on his belly. His T-shirt is twisted in a way that lets me see his skinny back. I think he forgets to eat when he's worried, but he still looks good.

And then there's his ass…. I stare at it a little bit too long, but he can't see my eyes, so it's okay. I shake my head in an effort to get my unwanted horniness under control, and I say, "My folks aren't about to let me out tonight, not after I was late coming home from cross-country."

Eleven months until I leave for college. I can survive eleven more months trapped in this split-level ranch prison with controlling parents who think they own me.

Do over—controlling parents who *actually do* own me.

"I'm going to try and call him again." Brody pulls his phone out of the back pocket of his jeans and presses D. "It's on speaker."

The ringing starts, and I have no expectations that Danny will answer, but Brody sweats out each ring. I sit down on the edge of the bed, drop my hand onto the base of his neck, and say, "Don't worry, Brody. I'm sure he's fine," even though I'm not, because tons of bad shit happens to Danny. Bad shit is a regular part of his daily routine. Under my hand Brody's neck muscles feel tight. I want to rub them until he relaxes. But I just let my hand lie there like it's not attached to the rest of my body.

"Hello."

Brody's so surprised to hear Danny's voice that he flips over and stares up at me, his eyes wide. "Danny-boy, what's going on with you? You've been totally off the radar—"

"In other words," I interrupt, "what the fuck, Danny? We've been going crazy trying to get in touch with you."

Silence. *Not* comforting. And then Danny's wiseass voice. "I take it I'm on speakerphone?"

"Yeah… so explain, Danny. I mean it." Brody's not goofing around.

"Jesus, take a chill pill, Decker." His voice is high-pitched and squeaky. Guilty. "It's just that my boyfriend…."

"That thug fry cook is your *boyfriend* now?" I'm yelling. I hate it that I'm yelling.

"Maybe. And he—look, Jared says he loves me… and I like it when he says that. I like it a lot. I don't want to piss him off, so… well, you guys know what I mean."

Jared says he loves Danny? Mom and Dad say they love me every morning and night. Sometimes I think "I love you" is just another tool to control me. What's the big deal with a stupid "I love you"?

"What did you do that pissed Jared off?" Like always Brody is focused on getting the facts. I should be too, but I'm busy wondering why a simple "I love you" from a virtual stranger is so important to Danny Denisco.

"He gets mad when I…." Danny seems to change his mind about finishing his thought.

"He gets mad when you do what?" Brody persists.

"It's like this—Jared won't let me spend all my free time with you guys. He says it's like I'm cheating on him and…."

"And?" Brody's so calm. I should be calm.

"And he says if I love him, I'll do what he wants, and if I don't, we're toast." Danny's voice is still high-pitched and a little whiny. It's like *he's* not even buying what he's trying to sell us.

"What the fuck?" I rub my ears because I can't believe what I just heard. There are still a few grains of sand in them from that windy afternoon at Branton Beach.

"Dude, we're *friends*. There's nothing wrong with the three of us hanging around together," Brody explains with more patience than I could ever scrape up. "And if this Jared person cares as much as he says, he won't tell you who you can and can't be friends with."

"I know, but he says he loves me… and that I'm the hottest guy in town."

"Well, at least the asshole's got good eyesight." I try to be funny, but it's wasted effort. Brody's the funny guy. "What I mean is, he's right." That part is truthful. Danny's got the prettiest blue eyes I've ever seen. Maybe nobody ever tells Danny that kind of sappy shit, and he wants to hear it.

There's more silence on Danny's end, and I'm not sure if my compliment flew right over his head. But when I look at Brody, he's staring at me. I don't think *he* missed my compliment. Then in this bright, too-cheerful voice, he says, "So, Danny, we'll still hang out together, but we'll keep it on the down low. How's that?"

More silence from Danny's end.

And all the silence is tough to take.

"But, dude," Brody adds, "you've got to let us know you're okay. No more disappearing acts. Fair?"

"Fine. I'll answer my phone from now on, so you guys don't freak. And we can hang out in school. No worries." Danny's reply is less than satisfying to me, but Brody smiles.

I don't know how Decker can keep his cool. One third of our friendship equation is bailing on us. If I didn't know any better, I'd think somebody stuck a knife in my upper left gut. Getting dumped physically hurts. I want to ask Danny "What the fuck?" again, but Brody sends me a stern "keep your mouth shut" look, so I do.

"Anyway, Danny, we'll catch up with you at lunch tomorrow." I can hear the smile in Brody's voice, so I know that Danny can also hear it on the other end of the call.

"K." Danny's voice is tiny. "Night, guys."

As soon as Brody ends the call, I stop trying to control my fury. "What the fuck is he thinking, Decker? What about all our plans, like the corn maze next weekend? And… and the three of us all going to Prospect University? What about *that*?"

Brody sits beside me and drops his legs over the edge of the bed. "Danny's not acting right. We both know it. So even if he says he can't hang out with us as much as usual, Perky, he needs us more than ever now."

"Henry, I think it's about time your friend went home," Mom shouts up the stairs.

"Your mother never refers to me by my name," Brody states, observant as always.

He's right. I think Mom chooses not to get to know Brody because she just plain doesn't like what he stands for. In her eyes, Brody's biggest failing is that his family doesn't go to church on Sundays. But there's so much more. He's not a jock, although he's as athletic as anyone I know, and he's not a brain, though he's smarter than our class valedictorian. And he's supposedly not a joiner, but he spends more unofficial time with the cross-country team, the Interact Club, Amnesty International, the Gay-Straight Alliance, the Lunch Bunch, and Special Olympics Club than any of their official members. Mom also calls Brody "a loose cannon" and says he's nothing but a distraction for me. But what it comes down to is that Brody can't hide his free spirit, and my parents want me to associate with people who live life inside the lines.

"Well, Mom knows I need to get my beauty sleep," I reply, again reminded that someday very soon, my folks will want to address my choice of friends—a pissed-off gay Goth kid and an adrenaline junkie.

"You don't need beauty sleep. You're beautiful enough." Brody's eyes are honest.

In a split second, I'm sweating and fighting against my urge to grab him and hug him.

Brody stands up and glances at the bedroom door. "I'll head out now and pick you up in the morning. But like ten minutes later than usual, because we won't have to go get Danny afterward."

"That sucks."

"Take my word on this, Henry. Danny's not leaving us for good." He takes a deep breath and repeats what he told me before. "He's going to need us more than ever... and soon. I know it."

"You got one of those inner feelings?" I ask.

Brody shakes his head. "Nope. I just know that an asshole like Jared is going to hurt a sweet kid like Danny sooner rather than later. There's no way around it. So you and I have to wait around to pick up the pieces."

Brody's notebook

TUESDAY, SEPTEMBER 23

Memoir of a Stalker—I sincerely hope this is only a temporary title.

I'm not exactly a stalker, but when it comes to Danny and Henry, sometimes I play the part of one.

And the situation with Danny is seriously messed up. I keep telling Henry that it will sort itself out. I hope I'm not lying to him.

Before I picked up Henry for school today, I drove by Danny's apartment building three times. Or maybe it was five times. I lost count.

Extremely stalkeresque.

I stared at the building each time I drove by, but there was nothing out of the ordinary—one beige cement building, nine nondescript windows with torn screens, five crumbling brick steps leading to a cracked plate glass door, zero landscaping. The place is almost invisible in its plainness. The only thing that draws any attention to the residence is the number of beat-up SUVs, ancient boats on trailers, and motorcycles that have seen better days that surround it. The property looks like a used-vehicle auction lot.

The first three times I passed by, I saw a couple of wrinkled old men with bloated bellies smoking cigarettes on the front walkway. I also noticed about five skinny cats skulking around the property. But no Danny. I was tempted to park behind the row of overgrown shrubs on the corner and wait as long as it took to see if he emerged alone or arm-in-arm with Jared, the jealous fry cook.

But I didn't stop. I passed by unnoticed… unless Danny happened to glance out the window. Lime-green Jeep Wranglers are hardly stealthy.

There's no valid reason for me to be snooping on him. Danny Denisco is not my boyfriend. He's not my best friend's boyfriend. We're straight. He's gay. The whole romance thing is not possible.

Danny's not a mystery I need to solve. He's just a guy from the bad part of town who happens to enjoy the darker side of life. He has an extraordinary gift for painting fluorescent sunsets on black velvet without making them look redneck tacky. His poetry could even bring tears to Lionel Wagner's eyes.

Danny has a fashion sense that, on a good day, could be called peculiar. Most of the time, Danny comes to school looking like a boy witch. He has multiple piercings in his ears, nose, bottom lip, right eyebrow, and probably other places I don't want to know about. Add to that an emo haircut, complete with sideswept bangs and neon-blue tips, and way too much black eyeliner.

That's Danny.

Like I said, no mystery.

Danny defines "gay, emo, Goth boy."

He looks radical, but he just wants what everybody else wants out of life.

And Danny is not my boyfriend. I don't know how I feel about that.

AFTER I stalked Danny, I drove to Henry's house to pick him up. Like always his mother followed him onto the front porch, questioned him aggressively about something or other, and then kissed his cheeks. I snickered, which might sound mean. Maybe I was jealous because *my* parents were up at five and out the door before six, without so much as a "see ya later, sonny," so they could attend aqua-aerobics class at the Nifty After Fifty Gym.

I wish I were joking about its name.

Henry was still blushing from Mommy's kisses when he got into the Jeep.

"You sleep okay?" I asked him. I remember that his eyes looked tired.

"I slept fine," he lied. "Any word from Danny?"

I shook my head when I said, "No worries. It won't be long until he's back." Again I wondered if I was inadvertently lying.

Henry looked at me with those tired eyes and said, "Whatever," which is really one of Danny's words.

There was so much hurt in Henry's expression. It made me wonder exactly what it is he feels for Danny. And then I wondered what I feel for Danny... and what I feel for Henry... and God knows that wasn't a direction I wanted my brain to go in. So I burned a strip of rubber on the street in front of his house and created a piercing screech and a cloud of dark smoke.

Mrs. Perkins still watched from the porch, and I knew it.

Henry shrugged, waved at his mother, and then asked me, "Why do you *do* shit like that?"

I didn't answer him. Henry doesn't need to understand that I'd do just about anything to stop obsessing over emotional stuff that gets in the way of my sanity—stuff like what it is I feel for my two best friends.

He gave me the silent treatment, though, until I said, "Sorry, Perky. Peeling rubber in front of your house was an accident." This was a blatant lie. So to make it more convincing, I added, "I just didn't want to be late for school." And that was an even bigger lie.

We both knew it.

Henry: My life

DANNY SITS across from us at lunch. He doesn't say too much. He doesn't laugh at our lame jokes. He doesn't take a single bite of the crappy chicken burger, tater tots, or tired-looking celery sticks on his brown tray, not that I can blame him. Danny just sits there, his eyes shifting back and forth from Henry to me. And we goof around like two losers and try to pretend everything's fine.

But Brody and I know things are much more wrong than right. Something bad that we know nothing about is going on between Danny and the asshole fry cook. Since we don't know what it is, we've got no clue how to fix it.

Free verse poetry by Danny D

"Henry runs"
Grasping speed with arms that rip and tear,
Hands, like claws, shred the late-day air.
Long legs straining, thigh muscles taut,
Teeth gritted, neck tight, lips twisted in a knot.
Sleek skin of brown,
Sweat dripping down….

Can I chase his spirit—a soul so fierce and free?
Can I steal his power—no longer to be me?
I want to drink his adrenaline,
I don't care if a race I win.
I can chase and claw, grit and strain—
Is there room for two in the fast lane?

Henry: My life

DANNY DOESN'T show up at today's home cross-country meet. I rationalize his absence by telling myself that cross-country isn't much of a spectator sport. But my parents are there, and Brody is too. Danny's never missed a meet before.

I will not let this affect my race. Yeah, right.

I don't believe that promise for a second, but the team has already done a group stretch, so I need to start thinking strategy.

25

"Hey, bud. Are you ready to run?" Brody always chats with me right before I race. It's a race he should be running too, and giving me some serious competition, but it isn't because he's not a "joiner."

"Yeah, I guess."

"Tell me. What's your plan?"

"The Wildcat's top runner isn't much of a sprinter. I'm gonna stay right behind him until the hill on Linden Street. When I get to the top, I'm gonna sprint to the finish."

"Sounds good. You think Lionel is going to be a factor in this race?"

"Lionel's always a factor. He pushes hard early, and it gets under my skin to see him break away. But I usually end up overtaking him at about mile two or so."

"And that's exactly what's going to happen today. No worries, Henry. You've got this."

He doesn't mention that Danny is a no-show. "Thanks, Bro." I wish like hell he was running too, even if he beat me. "Where are you gonna be?"

"Where do you want me?"

A loaded question. "How about at the top of the Linden Street hill?"

"I'm there."

"Okay. Gotta go."

Brody nods and walks in the direction of my parents, who act like they don't see him when he waves. To cover his embarrassment, he pretends he's playing with the blond spikes sticking up off his head, and he sprints down the road in the direction of the hill.

My face gets hot. I'm pissed off at Mom and Dad. I take a deep breath and blow it out slowly to push away the anger I'm not supposed to feel.

I'M NOT on my game. I've got no rhythm. Lionel's still out in front of me, as are the Wildcat's first and second runners. By the time I hit the bottom of the hill, I'm short of breath. I look up ahead and see Brody gazing down the hill at me. He's clapping and yelling, "You've got this, Perky. Now work the hill."

The sound of his voice focuses me. I close my eyes for a second and concentrate.

"Stay relaxed, like we do in practice."

I visualize Brody and me climbing Linden Street hill side by side, totally chill, like we do almost every day. When we race up together, it's fun, and it's no big deal... maybe because Brody isn't actually on the team, and he isn't an official competitor. More likely I know that he wants me to conquer the hill as much as I want him to.

"There you go. You got your rhythm back. Now's the time to turn it on!"

I glance at Brody as I pass him. I can tell he's fighting an urge to run along beside me, to encourage me until I cross the finish line.

I get a warm feeling in my gut and then a burst of new energy. Without too much trouble, I pass Lionel and the other team's number-two runner. There's only the Wildcats' top runner in front of me, and I can see him. I break into my sprint, and soon I'm running beside him. For a few long seconds, we run side by side, but I've got more to give. I pull ahead and cross the finish line three seconds before my competitor.

Once I step onto the grass, I have to bend over and put my head below my waist to catch my breath. Between my legs, I see my parents coming up behind me. I know I made them proud, which feels good. When I stand up again, Mom hugs me and Dad gives me a thumbs-up.

"I'm proud of my boy. So proud," Mom says as she hugs me around the neck. "Let's take a moment to thank the Lord for your athletic gift." She bows her head.

"You did a good job, Henry, but you didn't shave even a second off your time." Dad bows his head too, but also looks at his watch. "Well, there's always next time."

I'm distracted, and not by Dad's lukewarm congratulations or Mom's public prayer. I scan the crowd for the two faces I need to see. In the distance Brody jogs up the hill. He grins like a fool and sticks his fist in the air because he knows I won the race. I look around again, and in the woods behind the place where my mother's minivan is parked on the street, I see Danny. He's like a ghost, hidden in the trees, looking pale in his black shirt. And his eyes are too dark. Something's wrong with his eyes.

I look around for Brody again, but can't see him anymore. So I break out of Mom's embrace and race toward the woods.

"Son, you're acting rude." I hear disbelief in Dad's voice.

"Where are you going, Henry?" Mom calls. "Come back here this instant! We weren't finished thanking Jesus."

It kills me to stop and turn around. "Mom, I think I saw someone I know. I'll be right back." But when I turn back toward the woods, Danny's gone.

CHAPTER 3
THERE'S AN ELEPHANT IN THE ROOM

Henry: My life

"I SWEAR I saw him." I can't let it go. "Right after the race, he was standing in the woods on the side of the road." Brody and I are on the phone for the fifth time tonight.

"You're sure he had a black eye?" Brody's worried. I'm glad I'm not alone in freaking out.

"At least one—but maybe both eyes."

"I'm honestly not sure what to do, Henry. I called him ten times while you and your parents were out to dinner."

"I texted him from the restaurant's bathroom, right after I texted you. And I emailed him when I got back. He's avoiding us, just like he promised he wouldn't."

Brody's quiet. He's deep in thought. Usually he knows exactly what to do next, but he's being really careful.

"I can sneak outta my house after my parents go to sleep. And you can pick me up at the corner of my street, and then we can go to Danny's house and make sure he's okay," I offer, although the idea of doing that scares me. Mom and Dad wouldn't stand for it if they caught me. They'd never allow me to see Brody and Danny again.

Still nothing from Brody's end.

"Say something, dude."

"He told us that he didn't want to hang out, other than in school. So I think we should respect his request that we stay away, at least until

29

tomorrow. If he's not at school, we'll track him down. And if he shows up at school with a black eye or two, we'll find out what happened and do something about it."

"Okay. Okay, that'll work. And Brody, I think you were right."

"Right about what?"

"About Danny. You said that he was gonna need us, and it would be soon."

"I guess I did say that." He doesn't sound overly psyched about being right.

Free verse poetry by Danny D

"Mom"
i sit alone

bottles replace me; false substitutes for "we"
liquid joy and tears and passion and pride
spill between her lips,
soaking up the time
that should, by rights, be mine....
she says it can't be fixed

she sits alone

in her mirror a reflection: an image of the broken son
liquid sorrow falls from eyes that can't be dried....
the mirror slips... there's shattered glass,
and dry eyes seek to find
just one more gulp of wine—
the liquid nerve within her grasp.

I am shattered too

Brody's notebook

THURSDAY, SEPTEMBER 25
~~The Never-ending Journal~~
N is for notebook; that's good enough for me.
Danny wasn't in school today, which wasn't much of a surprise.

During lunch Henry went to see Coach Wentworth about missing cross-country practice. I think he told Coach that he had a massive migraine, and since Coach is still on a high from the week's big win, he let Henry skip. I wonder if he thought something was up when he noticed I wasn't at practice either.

We didn't waste any time getting over to Danny's apartment building after school. But when I pulled out of the high school parking lot, I didn't do it with a squeal, because I couldn't afford to get stopped by the cop who directs traffic when school lets out. Officer Steady likes to make a big show of his belief that safe driving begins in the parking lot—blah, blah, blah—and maybe he has a point. In any case I crawled out of the school lot and refrained from burning rubber when I pulled onto School Street, even though I could have used a distraction.

On the short ride to Danny's place, Henry and I didn't have much to say to each other. Henry committed the mortal sin of biting his nails. His father would shit a brick if he saw. I've heard Mr. Perkins tell Henry, "Confident young men don't stick their fingers in their mouths." Maybe comments like that explain Henry's lack of confidence.

I parked in the lot behind the building, between a trailer holding two 1980s-era snowmobiles and a tired, gold Honda Civic with no windshield or license plates.

Henry and I got out of the Jeep more slowly than we should have, seeing as Jared could have chained Danny to the radiator and might be beating him senseless. We went around to the front of the building and, as usual, the thick, glass security door wasn't working. So we walked right in and climbed the stairs to the third floor. When we got to Danny's apartment door, Henry pointed in my face. Naturally *I* knocked.

"We don't want none," I recognized Danny's mother, Christina's, voice. She sounded drunk, which was not unusual.

Since I'm always the one to do the talking when it comes to adults, I answered, "We aren't selling anything, Christina. It's Brody and Henry, and we're here to see Danny."

A few seconds later, the door cracked open about three inches, and we heard Christina say, "Daniel ain't home. I been on this couch all day, and I never seen him once."

Nonetheless I asked her if we could come in and check his room. I had a strong feeling he was in there.

The door flew open and banged into the wall. "Be my guest." She said it in the same snippy tone Danny would have used, and then she shuffled back to the couch. Evidence of her drinking binge covered the coffee table. There were a couple of empty wine bottles, but no glasses, and a half-dozen crushed-up beer cans. They were pretty much flattened. She must have anger issues too.

Henry mouthed the words "sucks for Danny" as we tiptoed across the living room and down the hall to Danny's bedroom. Again he pointed at me. Henry must think I'm the only one who knows how to form my hand into a fist and knock. But I did what needed to be done.

Danny replied without any delay to my knocks, so I figured he'd been listening at the door. "I can't see you guys right now."

Henry dove for the doorknob, frantically tried to turn it, and shouted, "It's locked, Decker! It's locked! Danny's door is fuckin' locked!"

He kept saying it until Danny came back with, "I can hear you, Henry… and yeah, the door's locked 'cause I wanna be alone."

I tried to engage Danny in conversation. "You weren't in school today."

From behind the door, I heard, "Duh. That's because I'm sick."

"You weren't too sick to come to my cross-country meet yesterday!" Henry shouted right at the door, and I thought, for a cool guy, Perkins has no idea how to fake calm. He kept going too. "And you have black eyes. I saw your face. I want to know how you got them."

Christina didn't want to hear our noise. She yelled down the hall, "Keep it down or you fellas are gonna have to go!"

"Sorry, Christina. We'll be quiet," I called back, and put a finger in front of my lips to remind Henry that we were guests in their apartment. And then I put my attention back on Danny and asked him one more time to let us see him.

He sounded upset when he again told us he couldn't let us in. Because of the staggered way he was breathing, I thought maybe he'd been crying. And I knew right then that whatever was going on with him and Jared had to be bad. "Anyways I dumped you guys as friends. I told you my boyfriend was my top priority and that you guys had better just learn to live with it. So why do you even give a crap?"

Henry made a choking sound, so I spoke for both of us. "Look buddy, we're seriously worried about you," I said, starting to feel really weird about the heavy conversation I was holding with a door.

"*Buddy*—ugh. Maybe that's the friggin' problem." Danny sounded defeated, but he rambled. "Being buddies, it's so not... like... not what I'm after. So why don't you *good buddies* get the hell outta here? Just go."

That was when Henry forgot all about keeping quiet, jerked at the door handle like a madman, and yelled, "Let us in! Let us in!"

It was like a miracle when the door slowly swung open. Danny stood in front of us wearing this strange, old-fashioned, white-nightgown thing he must have found at a thrift shop, because they sure don't sell them at the outlet mall where I shop. If he were clutching a candleholder, he would have looked like an orphan in a Dickens' novel. Danny's fine black hair was rumpled and stuck to his head, and, like Henry said, his eyes were both blackened and swollen. His bottom lip was puffy too.

"What the fuck?" Henry didn't shout it. He just asked. Then he rushed to Danny and hugged him. I couldn't see Danny at all because he was engulfed in Henry's embrace, so I used the time to collect myself. I'm the one who's supposed to keep my act together. I swallowed over and over until the lump in my throat went away, and when Henry finally let Danny go, I closed the door and told them to sit down on the bed.

Danny was oddly obedient. He took Henry's arm and led him to the bed. While they pushed back the rumpled sheet and blankets and sat down, I stood in front of them and asked, "What happened to you, Danny?"

He said, "Nothing," flopped back on the bed, and pulled a pillow over his head.

So I asked again, "What happened to your face?"

The pillow muffled Danny's voice, but it sounded like he said, "It's not just my face." Henry reached down and pulled the nightgown up to Danny's knees. His legs were covered in cuts and bruises, as though he'd been kicked in the shins too many times to count.

"I'm gonna fuckin' kill him." I think Henry was the one to say this, but it could as easily have been me.

When I suggested we call the cops, though, Danny popped up off the bed, waved at us, and said, "Um… hello. You guys are not gonna do either of those things 'cause I just wanna forget he did this to me."

And one more time, I questioned him, "So Jared did this?"

"Yeah, but I deserved it." Danny's answer floored me.

It caught Henry by surprise too. "What the fuck, Danny?"

I tried to explain how wrong Jared was, but it took me two tries. Finally I managed to say, "Look, Danny, you don't deserve this. Nobody deserves to get beat up."

When I finished speaking, Danny stared at Henry. And he made a confession. "Jared told me I couldn't go to your cross-country meet, but I said I wasn't gonna take no for an answer."

IT COULD HAPPEN

Henry pulled Danny back down beside him, and said, "You got beat up because of me."

I'm not sure why, but this makes me think of the day we met—PE class, fall of freshman year. Henry had just switched from the local Christian middle school to the public high school. And the kid had everything going for him. He's a big guy, cute in the girls' eyes, athletic, smart, and cool. If he wanted to, he could have owned Thomas Bailey Aldrich High School. But Henry wasn't into that kind of thing. His personality was just off-center enough to make him socially different, like Danny and me.

When he saw me struggling to show the awkward kid I always got stuck partnering with how to return a badminton serve, Henry came over to us, and without even a hello, taught Danny just how to hit the birdie. When Danny finally got it, we thanked him, and he stuck around for the rest of gym class. The three of us saw one another at lunch later that day, and we gravitated to the same cafeteria table.

That was the start of an epic friendship—the jock, the gay boy, and the kid with a few screws loose. It sounds like a triple stereotype, and maybe it is....

Anyway, I stood in Danny's bedroom, faced with the certain knowledge that his boyfriend had abused him. There were things I still needed to know. So I asked, "Do you think Jared's going to come back here and hurt you again?"

Danny shook his head and told me that Jared was done with him.

"You're done with him too, I hope." Henry again put into words exactly what I was thinking.

"I guess I'm done." Danny dropped his hands to his lap and thought aloud, "Maybe I didn't really love him. Maybe I was just glad he loved me."

"He didn't love you." Henry and I said it at exactly the same time. We caught eyes but didn't punch each other's arms and say, "Jinx ya," like we normally do when we speak in unison.

Danny said, "Whatever," and he stood up and turned to face us. It was hard to look at his eyes and lip, all swollen and bruised.

But Henry wasn't finished. "Just answer one thing for us, 'kay?"

Danny again agreed more readily than I expected.

"Why do you go out with so many guys you hardly even know, when you've got us to hang with?" Henry cut to the heart of the matter.

First Danny mumbled something about how we wouldn't get it and crossed the room to stand in front of his bureau. He glanced into the round mirror on the wall above it and pressed on the puffy skin beneath his right eye and then his left, as though he were checking melons for ripeness.

"Try us," I insisted.

Danny couldn't keep still. When he stepped back from his bureau and walked toward the bedroom door, I figured he was looking for an escape hatch, which I could fully relate to. But he finally explained himself. "I need the kind of feeling that comes from somebody who wants me as more than a friend. And this is probably gonna sound twisted, but Jared being jealous *proves* he loves me." He turned around and said to our faces, "There's no way you guys are gonna get it. I'm wasting *my* breath and *your* time."

Neither of us moved a muscle, because we knew Danny had more to say.

And he didn't disappoint. "I need to be close with a guy—to feel like he sees me as his. It makes me feel… like… it makes me feel secure, I guess."

Henry's reaction was in no way cool. "Jared beating you up makes you feel secure? That's warped." And then he took a huge risk. "Besides, you've already got that kind of closeness with us, dummy."

Danny sighed and asked Henry in a snippy voice, "Didn't you hear a fucking word I just said?"

"I heard every single fucking word." He glanced at me, maybe for reassurance, which he didn't get, and said, "And I'm telling you that you got me and Brody to be close to."

Danny reacted just like I expected. "Earth to Henry. You guys aren't gay, and I am. This conversation is so fucked-up. Both of you should just leave." Danny sent Henry a glare capable of melting the iceberg that sank the Titanic. "Jesus."

I thought maybe Henry would just get up and leave, I'd follow him out the door, and the whole thing with the three of us would be over. But that's not what happened. Instead Henry and Danny got into a conversation that caused my inner Houdini to contemplate escape plans.

It started when Henry claimed that the three of us are way more than just ordinary friends. I swallowed back my "Oh my God" and just listened.

"Fine. So maybe we're really good friends." Danny seemed to agree until he added, "But that doesn't make us potential lovers."

Henry pushed. "You gotta admit we aren't like Lionel and Jamie. Jamie would steal Lionel's wallet if Lionel left it sitting on the lunch table and turned his back."

He got no argument from either of us, because he was right.

Then Henry pushed more. "Try to see it this way. How many friends try to all go to the same college—especially when you, Danny, would rather get a job, and Brody would be much happier scaling a cliff without a safety harness or swimming with piranhas in the Amazon? And I'll probably get a full athletic scholarship to a more competitive college. That's the stuff my folks' wet dreams are made of."

Danny wrinkled his nose when Henry said "wet dreams," but he still demanded, "Cut to the chase, Perkins. What do you mean?"

At that point, Henry looked about as uncomfortable as I'd ever seen him. He's not usually the one to break new ground in our relationship. And the next thing he said was life changing for all of us. "I'm suggesting... that we give it a try." He glanced down at his feet, took a deep breath, and then said it again, but clearer. "That we give... *us*... a try."

His suggestion nearly knocked me over. The guy hasn't got the balls to knock on Danny's bedroom door for an uninvited visit, but he's got what it takes to suggest that we risk our friendship by putting romance, and all the shit that goes with it, between us.

And then the elephant in the room—there are three of us.

Henry: My life

I'M STILL in shock that I just suggested we give the possibility of us getting together as more than just friends a try.

Danny's wigging out right along beside me. He shakes his head and says, "This is so totally fucked-up."

I look at Brody. He's staring at me, sort of dazed. Usually he's the one to pull Danny and me out of the fire, but right now the flames are at his feet too. And if he's in close proximity to too much emotion, Brody takes a detour.

"Look. It's not as fucked-up as you guys might think." I get up off the bed and just stand there. Having no clue where my sudden courageousness and stupid honesty come from, I look from Brody to Danny and further turn our world upside down. I admit what I've known for a long time. "I'm gay."

"Holy shit." Danny loses it. "Holy. Freaking. Shit."

"Say something, Brody." Again I'm honest. "Your silence is freaking me out."

I can tell by his expression that Brody *wants* to pull us out of the building I've set afire with my excessive candor. "Uh… all I can say is… is…."

Nothing. Brody's got nothing. So I look from Brody to Danny and put my foot in it again. "So… uh, you guys wanna try it?"

"Jesus." Danny looks wide-eyed, like he swallowed one of those oversized gumballs. "Even if I did, nobody has *two* boyfriends."

In response, I nod, Danny shrugs, and Brody takes a deep breath and asks, "But the thing is—why not?" The words seem to pop out of Brody's mouth and surprise all three of us. "Why can't three people fall in love? As far as I know, there isn't a law against it."

Brody looks as if he might barf, but I still ask, "Are you for real? Are you saying you *want* to try to get closer?"

"Um… *hello*! Brody isn't even gay, like you suddenly *claim* to be, Henry." I'm the lucky recipient of Danny's withering glare. "This entire conversation is whack. It's whack, and it can't be real. So let's get real right now."

I've developed a one-track mind over the past ten minutes, though, and before I think it over, I ask *again*, "So are you guys in?" My mother would have kittens if she knew what I'm suggesting. What I'm pushing so hard for.

Finally Brody has something to say. "It isn't that simple for me, Henry."

"Uh, dude," I say. "A gay threesome is not what I'd call simple at all."

Danny giggles because he's nervous. I get where he's coming from and fake a little laughter too.

But Brody doesn't even smile. He just gets up off the bed and walks out of Danny's bedroom.

"What the fuck, Brody?" I follow him into the hallway. "Where the hell are you going?"

It's too late to get an answer. Decker's already checked out, in the mental sense. He rushes past Christina, who appears to have passed out on the couch, and he's out the door.

I GO back into Danny's bedroom and tell him, "Get some pants on, dude." Once he's wearing skinny jeans and has replaced the weird nightgown with a black sweatshirt, I grab him by the wrist, and we follow Brody from the apartment. But he's got a dangerous head start.

"If he gets in his car right now, he's likely to go one hundred and ten down Main Street," Danny says as we cross the living room. "He'll kill himself or somebody else, and then he'll kill himself because he killed somebody else." Strangely Danny's nonsensical statement makes complete sense. "We've got to stop him, Henry."

We run down three sets of stairs and out of the building, down the walkway, and around to the back lot. When we get to the parking lot, we see Brody's Jeep parked in the same spot and breathe a mutual sigh of relief.

"Brody's on foot," I observe, and we both yell his name into the woods behind the lot. After ten minutes of our yelling met with Brody's silence, we know he's either not able to hear us or he's ignoring us, so we head to the Jeep. The top is off, and when we look inside, we see the keys on the passenger seat. "I think Brody was worried I'd miss my curfew if he took the Jeep. He left the keys so I could drive myself home."

"Your stupid curfew probably saved Brody's life," Danny notes.

"I hope so."

"What do we do now?"

"I guess we settle in and wait for him," I say, and we climb inside.

Brody's notebook

THURSDAY, SEPTEMBER 25

I'm back and this time without a clever new idea for what to officially call this notebook. Maybe whatever name I give this notebook doesn't even matter, but I'm a detail-oriented guy. I appreciate the little stuff in life.

Nonetheless I'm going to skip forward now and write about how I ran.

When things got to be too much for me in Danny's bedroom, I took off. I had a need to get the hell out of there, as well as a need for speed, so I bolted.

At first I thought I'd take my Jeep for a fast ride. I'd let the wind do its job and blow all the worries out of my head. But then I realized I'd be screwing Henry. He'd be stuck at Danny's house, would never make it home in time for dinner, and his folks wouldn't forgive him for a month. So I stuck the keys on the passenger seat and headed for the woods.

To outrun the feelings that barked at my heels, I raced through the forest. Trees blocked me, but I dodged when I could and let the stinging slap of branches across my skin distract me from fear of the pain I'd have to deal with if my emotions caught up with me. I heard Danny and Henry call me, but I couldn't go back. I needed to run, and that's what I did—so hard and fast I didn't notice that the wind kicked up until it finally stole my breath. The woods had turned dark and cold around me, so when I finally could breathe again, I slowed to a jog and headed back toward Danny's building.

I ran toward the friends I'd run from, knowing that I'd probably hurt them by taking off in the first place. As my feet pounded the matted leaves, I promised I would make it up to them. When I finally stepped out onto the dimly lit parking lot, I found my Jeep was still there with the top on, and Danny and Henry were safely out of the wind, waiting for me. I finally let myself feel the cold that chilled my bones and the scratches that stung my face.

I walked slowly to the Jeep's passenger side and peered in to see Henry and Danny in the front seat. When I knocked on the window, they didn't jump out of their skins, so I figured they expected me.

Danny rolled the window down, but I spoke to Henry. I said, "I left the keys on the seat so you could drive home. You're going to be up shit creek with your folks."

At that point they both stared at me in horror. Danny put what was in their eyes into words. "You look like a zombie after a meal. Jesus, Brody."

I remembered the branches that scratched my cheeks while I ran through the woods, so I licked my palms and rubbed the splotches of blood from my face.

Then I returned to my original point. "Henry, you seriously need to get home before your mother organizes a search party." I cracked a smile to lighten things up, but they refused to go with it.

"You were gone for like two hours," Danny said. He opened the passenger door, which forced me to step back, and he jumped down from the Jeep. "Come on," he said.

Henry got out too, but he came around the Jeep, put his hand on my shoulder, and informed me that I was going along with them.

As we walked toward the building, I reminded Henry, for the third time, of what he already must have known. "Your parents are going to think you got abducted by aliens."

He came back with, "I called home. Told them I have a major group project due tomorrow, and if they don't want me to get a C in Spanish they need to let me stay out later than usual tonight."

"And my mother passed out, so I put her to bed. We'll have no distractions when we talk."

"Great." I'm pretty sure I said that out loud, and it seriously lacked enthusiasm.

I followed them into the building and realized I had little choice but to face my feelings. As I walked I wished that *I'd* be abducted by aliens.

WHEN WE first came into the apartment, Danny took a couple of minutes to toss the empty bottles and cans into a grocery bag and wipe off the coffee table with a wet rag. The room still smelled like a bar, but it wasn't too bad.

They made me sit between them, probably to make sure I didn't take off running again. And Henry acted first. He grabbed my hand and then reached across me to take Danny's hand. When we were linked together like a paper-people chain, he sucked in a huge gulp of air… and then didn't say a thing. Typical.

Danny rolled his eyes and asked, "Henry mentioned something about… a threesome, right?"

I nodded as though it were a simple proposition—three dudes in love… in high school. Like that won't get us killed. I started sweating again, and it crossed my mind that emotional turmoil was an entirely new way for me to get an adrenaline rush.

Henry stared straight ahead, like he was trying to control his flaring emotions by disciplining the movement of his eyeballs.

But Danny didn't look as devastated as he did when we first saw him in the afternoon, when he stood in front of his bed in that old-fashioned nightgown and looked like the Ghost of Christmas Past.

42

He was in the mood to talk too, and he focused on me. "Brody, did you run off because you aren't into this? You know, because you're straight and—"

"No." I was too dazed to give a better answer. But I wasn't too dazed to think, and images of gay Henry and gay Danny making out and not-so-gay me standing alone on the sidelines watching them rushed into my brain. I shook my head and tried to make the images fall away.

"So you *don't* want to try this?" Henry asked me.

I shook my head again.

"Then you do?" It was Danny's turn.

There was a lot of noise in my head, but the loudest voice screamed, "I don't want them to do this without me." I knew I couldn't deal with being the third wheel on a bicycle when we'd always been a tricycle.

Finally I just said, "It could happen."

"Nobody does this kind of thing," Danny reminded us, as if we needed a reminder. "Like, nobody."

Right then something must have crossed Henry's mind that made his eyes widen and a strange snorting sound emerge from his throat. I wonder if he imagined the Jocks"R"Us lunch table's reaction to the *three* of us walking across the Thomas Bailey Aldrich High School cafeteria holding hands or the expression on his parents' faces when he told them that he was a member of a gay threesome.

He laughed wildly. It was very un-Henry.

I closed my eyes, swallowed hard, and out popped the only thing I could possibly say. "The three of us, together. I think it *could* happen."

Free verse poetry by Danny D

"Brody runs"
Once he ran into the woods
Where branches scraped his face

Leaving narrow stripes of blood
Visible etchings, engraved by fear
Of needing us
Of losing us
He cannot be still
When fear surges in his blood
Like the adrenaline of
A runner.

CHAPTER 4
GOING NOWHERE FAST

Henry: My life

I'M NEVER going to be able to fall asleep.

It's too damned stuffy in my room. Maybe I need some air.

Mom and Dad always open the windows in their bedroom at night, even if it's just a crack. They say God's gift of an evening breeze can be calming. So I kneel on my bed and push my window open about a foot. The cool nighttime air quickly soothes me.

This is just what I need. I guess Mom and Dad are right about some stuff.

I lie back down on my narrow bed, close my eyes, and try like hell to pull the imaginary brake in my brain that will stop the rush of thoughts. I yank it hard, but my brain brake malfunctions. It drags and squeals, but barely slows down the thinking train. It's clear I can't will myself into la-la land. So I sit up on my bed, switch on the light mounted on my headboard, and let my thoughts chug along.

This whole thing with Danny and Brody happened way too fast.

I'm not ready for it.

Who on earth would be ready for a gay threesome in high school?

Nobody sane.

But it was MY genius idea....

It feels good to finally admit I'm freaking out, especially when I know *I'm* mostly responsible for what's going to wreak havoc on a perfectly good friendship... and probably get me kicked out of

National Honor Society… and beaten silly in the locker room after basketball practice this winter. The options for my downfall are endless.

I pull the brain brake again. And again, it fails me.

I told Brody and Danny that I'm gay—a conclusion that's still up for debate.

No, the debate's been over for a long time now. I'm every bit as gay as Danny.

So it looks like I came out to my two best friends today.

Danny was skeptical, but for the most part, he was cool with it.

But Brody's straight. How's he supposed to be gay with us?

Brody said he was in, but he's gonna back out.

We're gonna lose him.

I'm gonna lose them.

Because this thing won't work with just two of us.

It's a threesome, or bust.

Shit on a shingle. I'm gonna lose both of them.

I'M CERTAIN I'm never going to fall asleep. This sucks because I have an away meet tomorrow. *How can I run three miles faster than everybody else and cut my time like Dad wants me to on absolutely zero sleep?*

There's only one person who can help me. I look at the clock on my phone. It's just past midnight, but he'll still be up. Brody's a total night owl.

I press B on my cell phone, and before Brody even says hello, I'm talking. "I thought I was ready for this, but, shit…. I think I really screwed up because—"

"Take a breath, Henry."

"But I came out to you guys, and I hadn't even decided for sure I was gay until the very second I said it…. but I *am* gay, and I'm freaking out that I ruined everything with us three, and I can't exactly unsay what I said and… shit." Talk about verbal diarrhea.

"Henry, did you hear me? I said that you need to breathe." He sounds sleepy. Maybe Brody actually *does* sleep like everybody else. "And you need to get some rest."

"I can't. I tried."

"Okay. That's cool. We'll talk for a while, until you get tired."

Just hearing his voice makes my breathing slow down, which I'm aware is fucked-up in itself. But Brody does that for me every single time I need him. He never fails. *How am I supposed to not fall for a guy who can do that?* "I shouldn't have said what I said today. I went and blew it."

"You said how you felt. That's not a crime, last time I checked." I have no idea how, but Brody's still calm.

"But dude, it changes shit with me and you and Danny."

He doesn't try to hide his long sigh. "Yeah, it does." Brody's voice is softer than usual, but I still hear him loud and clear.

It does? Oh God. It does.

"What the fuck have I done?" I lie down and roll onto my side so I face the window. "Did I ruin every fucking thing with us?"

Brody is silent for a split second too long.

I screwed up the best thing in my life.

I end the call. And totally freak out.

HALFWAY THROUGH my freak-out—which consists of a recitation of all the curses I know followed by panicked praying, one hundred sit-ups, fifty push-ups, and more praying—my window screen slides in on top of my bed and Brody's upper body plunges across the windowsill.

"What the fuck?" I'm not in the right mindset to get creative with my expletives.

"I'm here," Brody says brightly. "Could you pull me in the rest of the way?"

"Oh, yeah... of course." I grasp Brody's wiry forearms and yank. He slides through the window and ends up between the wall and me.

"I'm here," he says again.

He's so close to me that our arms are tangled and I can smell his Brody smell. And he's looking up at me with an expression that's probably as shocked as mine. When he shrugs he looks damn cute, but I don't let it distract me. I know what I have to do. "Listen, I made a big mis—"

"You don't have to take it back." Brody's suddenly serious. For some reason it hits me that I've never been able to figure out what color his eyes are, mostly because he never stays still long enough for me to really look at them. Right now, in my unlit room, his eyes look big and dark and very worried.

"What the fuck do you mean?"

"Don't take back what you said earlier tonight, Henry. About what you want to happen with the three of us."

"Don't worry, dude. I *can't* take it back 'cause it's what I want." I'm somehow compelled to be dangerously honest, just as I was earlier. "I *can* admit it was a mistake that I *told* you guys, though."

He clears his throat and says just what I don't want to hear, "I don't know if I'm gay."

"Shit," I reply.

"But I don't know how much that matters."

"Huh?" I ask.

"I'm kind of flexible, I think."

"Huh?" I ask again, but even louder, because I've got no clue what he's talking about.

"And I like to be with you guys. I want to be part of this... *this thing*."

"It's called a threesome, dude. A three-way gay *love* fest." I exaggerate the love part so he knows what he's getting himself into.

Brody smiles. "I love festivals." He really does. Brody always drags Danny and me off to places like Improv-apalooza at the Wellington Field downtown and Twin Rivers Acoustics Festival in South Hamstead.

"Be serious," I say. Brody's not serious about a lot, but I need him to be serious right then.

"I *do* love festivals," he insists, and then he's quiet, but I can't miss the holy-shit look in his eyes. I half expect him to dive back out the window, because whenever things get too sensitive, Brody gets gone. But he makes the effort to try and relax beside me and turns my way in an apparent effort to find a comfortable position. "I can't *not* try."

"But what about you *not* being gay?"

I expect him to assure me that he *is* a little bit gay, but he says something completely different. "That's not the problem for me. Not at all. The way I feel about you and Danny is strong, and I'm not really worried about being gay or straight. And gender isn't a big deal."

I'm not sure if I believe that Danny and me being guys isn't a factor in how Brody feels about us. How can it not matter? "So if it's not that we're dudes and you're into girls, what worries you about us getting together, then?"

He laughs. It's short and maybe a little snarky—a sound Danny might make—which surprises me, because Brody's always aboveboard. "What worries me?" he asks either himself or me. It's tough to say.

"Yeah. Spill it."

"What worries me is just being… just being open… about how I feel. Being open… in a *romantic* way, you know?" Brody, the perpetually chill dude, is sweating buckets. Literally. I can feel the moist heat radiating from his body. "I guess I'm not okay with gut spilling."

"But it's just with me and Danny. No one else has to know we're together." It occurs to me that Brody has a fear of intimacy or whatever he thinks intimacy is supposed to be. "And you don't have to be any different than how you always are."

"I could care less who knows that I'm into you guys." Brody looks up at me, and I decide his eyes are a very dark gray. "I think I can handle being the same 'pain in the butt' Brody with you guys, though, if that's all it takes to do this."

Brody still doesn't sound convinced, so I say, "That's all it takes."

He sighs again, but it's the good kind. "Can I stay with you tonight? I can wake up at five and go home before your parents ever see me."

Brody and I have been at sleepovers together plenty of times before. We usually stay at his house, and Danny's always there too. The three of us stretch out on his luxurious bed—always with Danny in the middle—but we never touch one another, unless it's by accident. And we like being physically close. Maybe we should have taken that as a strong clue as to how we felt about one another, but since Brody's bed is a California king, we could be close without having to actually cuddle up together.

It feels so different.

It's the first time Brody and I have been alone with each other in a bed and also the first time since we talked about our monumental relationship change.

"You can stay if you put the window screen back in the window," I say.

"Done." Brody goes to work and replaces the screen.

"Where are you parked?" I ask. I don't want a neighbor to tell my parents that Brody's lime-green Jeep Wrangler was parked on the street in front of our house overnight. They'd probably assume things… that are likely true.

"Don't worry. I'm parked in the woods, halfway down the trail to the pump house."

"Cool."

Brody still wears his jeans and T-shirt, but after he toes off his hiking boots, he seems comfortable enough. He sets the alarm on his phone and again settles beside me on my twin bed. I turn onto my side and face outward, and he turns in the same direction, right behind me. I can feel his breath on the back of my neck.

"Thanks for coming over tonight, Brody. I was freaking out."

"I knew you'd be freaking out. I figured I'd come here and talk you off the ledge." He yawns.

"You're good at that." I yawn too, because yawns are contagious. "I got the okay from Mom and Dad to sleep at your house on Saturday night."

"You did? That's awesome. It'll be the three of us." I can hear the smile in his voice, and smiles are contagious too. He presses the back of his hand against my forearm. It's not like he's trying to hold me, but I get to feel his skin on mine. It's perfect.

Grinning stupidly I nod, but he can't see it.

I'm sleepy.

We're almost spooning, I think and close my eyes.

Brody's notebook

FRIDAY, SEPTEMBER 26

~~*Perkins, Decker, and Denisco*~~

This title is not going to work. It sounds too much like the name of a funeral home.

And so now we're a gay threesome.

This is a carefully guarded secret. I'm pretty sure that even torture by waterboarding wouldn't get us to spill it. As we sat together today during lunch block B—at our regular table, in our regular seats, eating our regular lunch—the situation was anything but regular.

For the first time ever, Henry, Danny, and I were awkward in one another's company. In my head we had this weird exchange:

"How was your day, dears?"

"Fine, thank you."

"Fine, thank you."

"And yours?" Asked in unison.

"Well, I can't complain."

Weird.

In the real world, we sat in stony silence.

And what did we need to make the situation more awkward, if that was even possible? *I know, I know!* Harassment from the jocks' lunch table.

"Look, you guys—the Decker-Perkins sandwich cookie with the creamy Denisco filling is crumbling." This is a tough line to forget, and Lionel Wagner was unaware of how perfectly on-the-money his cookie-slander actually was. He had more up his sleeve too. Lucky us. "Whatsa matter, boys? Why the *straight* faces?"

No-neck Nelson called out, "Good one, Wags."

Danny rolled his eyes and then stuffed his hamburger into his mouth, probably to stifle a remark that would have gotten him beaten up in the parking lot after school. Henry clenched his teeth, puffed up his chest, and started to get up, but I talked him back down and reminded him, "Those guys don't matter, Perky. Let it go."

Henry was already close to his boiling point, which didn't bode well for the future prospects of our unconventional relationship. Judging by the fact that we haven't yet even started interacting as anything more than three awkward friends, he was slightly too worked up by a couple of rude remarks that were nothing but par for the course.

I had to think quickly, so I suggested, "Let's go out into the courtyard." Some space from the Jocks"R"Us lunch table was just what Henry needed to help him calm down.

Henry didn't nod or shake his head. He jumped up off his seat and stormed over to the trash barrels, dumped his untouched lunch, and stalked out the door. Danny and I glanced at each other and shrugged. Then we tossed everything except his hamburger and my veggie burger, choked them down, and followed Henry into the courtyard.

When we sat on the stone wall on either side of Henry, Danny was quick to go negative. "I think it'd be an understatement to say that our romantic threesome isn't off to a fabulous start. Maybe we should just dump this big fat gay idea."

That wasn't what Henry needed to hear. He literally growled.

Danny stood up and flipped the bird to somebody in the cafeteria, through the huge glass wall.

Things were going nowhere fast. It was time for me to do what I do best—talk the boys down. So I got into therapist mode. "Look, you guys. It's day one of something completely new to us. We shouldn't expect things to come together magically. It's going to take some work." Maybe I was playing the part of marriage counselor, but they listened. "Henry, do you think you can look the other way when Lionel is being… himself?"

Henry mumbled, "I can try."

"Good. It'll be worth it." I wore a fake smile and felt a lot like a game show host. "And Danny, I don't think we should get in the habit of jumping to the conclusion that this isn't working out before we've even given it a fighting chance."

"Whatever" was all Danny said. He isn't one to fall in line, but I'm pretty sure he heard me too.

For the record I have no idea who died and made me king of this threelationship. Wasn't I the last guy to sign on to this thing? And now it looks like I'm in charge of it. But Danny needs to feel secure, and Henry needs a lot of support. I'm good at giving them that stuff.

It came as a relief when Henry took our conversation in a different direction. "Wagner and his gang always fuck with my head on meet days. He's probably trying to get under my skin to screw me outta my win in Martinsville."

"It's like a conspiracy, huh?" Danny asked, and it took us back in time to when we were simply best friends. "You can fix his wagon by beating the snot out of him in the race today."

Henry and I laughed, and Danny smirked. I said, "Danny and I are going to drive to the meet. We'll take great pleasure in watching you kick Lionel's butt, so don't let us down."

I'd say we all felt close to normal at that moment, but who knows what's to come? I sure don't.

CHAPTER 5
A TOTALLY DYSFUNCTIONAL THING

Brody's notebook

SATURDAY, SEPTEMBER 27
   ~~*Go Ask Brody*~~
   Sometimes I think that Mom and Dad wouldn't notice if I up and disappeared. And I'm not trying to put them down, because my parents are great people, and I love them, and they love me.

The thing is my parents have been there and done that with regard to raising boys. They've gone to preschool parent's nights and T-ball games and tooth fairy visits and Boy Scouts badge ceremonies six times already. I think they were just tired when my turn came. So I'll rephrase the statement from above from "they love me" to "they love me, just not in a hands-on way."

Again, in their defense, of my six brothers, the one closest in age to me is eleven years older, which points to the fact that I'm the result of an "oops, dear" or more likely, a "Holy moly, Dottie" moment. Maybe one evening about nineteen years ago, Bernie and Dot had a little too much wine at dinner, one thing led to another, and next thing you know, here's Little Brody. I'm a realist, and I know that my conception was what you'd call unplanned.

Okay. My very existence is a complete and total accident. A mistake. Maybe a disaster.

I think what happened last night at dinner best illustrates my situation:

IT COULD HAPPEN

"Little Brody, be a dear, and slide the saltshaker down the breakfast bar, would you?" She sounded so sweet and innocent, but Mom is sly. "My goodness, I'm absolutely famished."

"I know what you're up to, Mom. And it's not going to work. 'Famished' or not, the doctor said no salt" was my response. I can be firm when I need to, even if they let me get away with murder.

"Dottie, Little Brody's right. Dr. Alpert cut your sodium intake at your last checkup, remember?" Dad then proceeded to pour a literal snowcap of salt on top of the mountain of cheese and bacon bits that smothered his first of three Wendy's baked potatoes. And he went on to add insult to injury, or at least I'm sure Mom saw it that way. "I'm glad you decided to pick up multiple potatoes for me, son. I didn't realize how hungry I'd be after all the walking we did at the golf course today."

Mom looked down at her lonely baked potato that was covered with nothing but a mound of unbuttered broccoli. She frowned. "No cheese or sour cream, Little Brody?" she asked and then made this tsk-tsking sound like she was disappointed in *me* because I was the one to fetch her dinner *exactly* as she requested it.

"I thought you were going to pour the plain yogurt over the potato," I reminded her. "I stopped at the Shopper's Mart to buy you some. And I got the fat-free kind, like you said."

She wrinkled her nose, but nonetheless saturated the potato in several heaping tablespoons full of yogurt. Then she threw me a curveball. "I suppose you're right, dear. And I'll be going off my dietary restrictions next weekend when we take the Seniors Tour of Salem."

I looked up from my potato. "What tour?"

"Did we forget to mention it to you, son?" Dad asked as he swallowed down the last bite of his second potato and scraped the black plastic carton with his fork to get every last trace of the cheese, in accordance with his "waste not, want not" policy. "Your mother and I are going on a bus tour with Eddie and Lois next weekend. It *is* October, after all, so it's time to start our fall recreational activities."

How could I forget? I've been my own babysitter for roughly five days in early October since I was in seventh grade. I, however, don't forget to tell *them* about critical stuff. "Remember, you said I could have friends over next Saturday night."

"Oh yes. Of course. Mrs. Perkins called a few days ago to make sure we'd be home. Silly me. I told her we'd be here. The trip to Massachusetts slipped my mind." Mom forgets a lot of things, but I don't think anything's wrong with her memory. It's more her motivation that's a problem. She asked me, "Should I call her back, you think? And tell her we're going to be away."

"Oh no," I replied quickly. "There's no need for that." Telling Mrs. Perkins that we won't be chaperoned would be a deal breaker.

Thankfully Mom was agreeable. "Good, because Lenore Perkins is a most unpleasant person, and I do not enjoy speaking with her. And I get a distinct feeling she's not enthusiastic about your friendship with Henry." And that's an understatement. If Perky's mom had it her way, I'd be banished forever from Henry's golden life.

"We're planning to leave on Thursday morning, son. So you'll need to be the man around the house until, say, the following Tuesday. But maybe you should make it Wednesday, to be on the safe side," Dad said with a wink.

"Not a problem," I told him and winked back.

"Finish eating that lovely potato now, Dot," he added. "It's almost time for bingo."

Mom grimaced, and then, after dousing what remained of her potato with olive oil spray, she finally dove into dinner and said, "I'm simply living for next weekend. I'm going to indulge, Bernie. There's a wonderful ice cream parlor down the street from our hotel, if I'm not wrong. Remember? I think it was called Lovin' Spoonfuls?"

I know I'm spoiled. A successful career in insurance for Bernard Decker and many smart investments later, cash is not a problem in my parents' retirement. And since they subscribe to the "you can't take it with you" school of thought, they live life high on the hog, a favorite expression of Mom's that I honestly don't get because hogs really aren't particularly tall. My folks have no problem sharing the wealth either. I drive the best vehicle of any kid in the high school. I have free use of my own credit cards and access to unlimited sums of cash. And "Little Brody's" bedroom? I basically have the entire third floor, which is so big it used to be the bunkhouse for *all* of my older brothers. Not only do I have my own bathroom and sitting room up there, I actually have a wet bar. And if I wanted a Jacuzzi tub in my oversized bathroom, one would be installed tomorrow.

So I *am* spoiled, if that means I get lots of stuff. Money is no object. I know that anywhere I want to go to college will be nothing but a patriotically designed Bernie Decker personal check away.

Which leads to the one way in which I'm not spoiled at all. I'd categorize it as a serious lack in both quality *and* quantity spent time with family. For example this is our first family meal in two weeks because Mom and Dad eat at five precisely. I'm not even back from cross-country at that point. I've never been asked to report to them with my report card, which might seem like a gift from God, but it doesn't serve to motivate me much at school. I only see my brothers on Thanksgiving and Christmas... when it's convenient for their families. And Dot and Bernie are gone more often than they're home. In fact number one on their bucket list is to "experience" each US state in the ginormous Winnebago that's wedged in the side yard between our house and the next-door neighbor's white picket fence.

But it's rotten of me to complain. Danny's mother is a complete alcoholic who passes out every night on the couch in their living room. And poor Henry is the subject of his parents' mutual obsession. I have it good.

I wasn't too interested in the baked potato, so I pushed the remainder forward and stuck my elbows on the breakfast bar. Nobody would think to tell me it was impolite. I watched as Mom polished off her tasteless-but-slick potato and headed to the bathroom to brush the broccoli out of her teeth, muttering something about how she wouldn't need to apply lip gloss because she could still feel the potato grease on her lips. Dad collected the trash and, without a thought to the environment, tossed it all into the trash can under the kitchen sink.

Another perk—no washing dishes when all I eat is take-out.

I do have a measure of "keep the earth green" guilt, though, so I pulled the Wendy's paper bags out of the trash and stuck them into our family's underused recycling bin.

I know I'm lucky. It could be so much worse.

"Good night, Little Brody," Dad said. I really have to nix this nickname before Henry and Danny catch on to it.

"And don't wait up for us. After bingo, we're going to the Town Tea Shak—it's open late now and anybody who's anybody from bingo goes," Mom informed me as she grabbed her purse off a barstool. "Come along, Bernie. We don't want to miss the beginning. The introduction of new players is the best part."

"They have no idea what kind of competition they're facing." Mom and Dad snickered like villains.

"Have fun, you guys," I said. "And take it easy on the newbies." So maybe I had a few things on my mind that I'd have liked to bounce off my parents—like whether friendship can grow so strong that it turns into love. Because I think that has happened to me.

But it wasn't the right time. Mom and Dad had places to go and bingo games to win. So I decided that it *was* the right time to take my mountain bike on a little trip down the three steep flights of stairs at city hall without laying so much as a single finger on the handlebars. I almost have that stunt mastered.

I headed to the garage and grabbed my bike, glanced at the dusty helmet on the floor, and like always, thought, "No can do." Mom and Dad never once wore bike helmets when they were kids, and they turned out fine.

Free Verse Poetry by Danny D

How did I end up here?

A rare blend of friendship and love should be mine,
but desperation of need makes me blind.

IT COULD HAPPEN

Lines of laughter should shape my eyes,
but valleys worn by tears are my prize.

How did I end up here?

I made a choice
to avoid the challenge of sailing unknown seas.
I made a choice
to settle for an ending that I could gain with ease.

Rather than the steep, curving, narrow climb to light,
I chose the well-worn slide, down the hill to pain and plight.

Henry: My life

"GET YOUR ass to the Food Pyramid. ASAP." This is the voice message, accompanied by an identical text message, that Brody will find whenever he gets his ass in gear and looks at his phone. Meanwhile, it's just Danny and me dealing with the bullshit. Thankfully we're not on school grounds, so if I end up killing that thug fry cook, Jared, maybe I'll go to jail, but I won't get suspended from Thomas Bailey Aldrich High School during cross-country season.

I step through the swinging doors at the far end of the restaurant and enter the backstage world of the Food Pyramid on Main Street, a mystery I had no urge to uncover. Danny and Jared are still over by the salad-prep area arguing. In my opinion they're way too close to a butcher block filled with black-handled knives for anybody's comfort.

"I didn't mean it was *over* over with us, baby." There's no doubt that Jared is good-looking. He's got that "I'm a dangerous bad boy" thing going on that probably begs Danny to fix him or mold him into something warmer and fuzzier or maybe just make him fucking smile.

Whatever it is that Jared's got, I don't give a shit at the moment. He hasn't got Danny, which is all that matters. I say, "Come on, Danny, go clock out, and we can call your boss and ask him about putting you and... and him... on different hours."

"Um... excuse me, but I don't think you work here, worm, so go back to wherever it is you slithered in from," Jared says to me, eyes still fixed on Danny. "Besides, can't you read? The sign says employees only."

"I don't give a shit what the sign says. Danny's coming with me." I can't resist adding, "And earthworms crawl. *Snakes* slither, you dumbass."

Danny doesn't seem to be convinced he should leave, though. His still-blackened eyes are focused on the hunky fry cook. "Look, Jared, you said we were over, so I moved on. It's that simple." His voice wavers.

"So you 'moved on'? You moved on with who? This slimy worm, here? Gimme a break." Jared sticks a thumb in my direction and laughs. "Now listen, baby. You and me, after work, we gonna go see Rob's band play in Gary's garage, and then we gonna party all night." He steps toward Danny and grabs him by the shoulders. "You're what I need *and* what I want, so shut the fuck up in advance, baby, if you gonna try to fight me on this one."

Danny is spellbound by the asshole. I actually think he's considering Jared's tainted offer. Danny looks like he's thinking, "Sure, why not? If you need me and want me, you sweet thug, then I'm all yours." He tugs at the front of his red apron and fiddles with the bright blue ends of his hair, but doesn't say a word.

Most notably, in my mind at least, Danny doesn't say, "Stuff it up your ass, old man, and stop calling my boyfriend a worm," the way I want him to.

I can't let Danny get back together with Jared for a crap load of reasons, most important, Danny's safety. So I push aside the hurt that Danny would even *consider* going with him—especially since we're together—and I focus on making sure it doesn't happen. I might be a worm, but I'm six inches taller than Jared, and I've got maybe fifty pounds on him, so I have no fear of stepping up in his face. "He's not going anywhere with you tonight." I speak as calmly as I can, but I feel the fury surge through my veins. "So lay the fuck off Danny and start frying mozzarella sticks or whatever it is you do back here. Otherwise there's gonna be trouble."

Danny's nervous as hell, so he makes the mistake of snickering, and all hell breaks loose. I'm relieved that Jared doesn't grab one of the knives from the butcher block, but our fists still start to fly. His flailing swings are easy to duck, and I manage to get a few good punches in on his left ear and jaw that seem to stun him. Soon he squeezes me around the shoulders and tries to drag me to the ground.

I can hear Danny shriek, although through my adrenaline haze, he sounds like he's a mile away. "Stop fighting, you guys. Stop it, right now!" As Jared and I drop to the sticky linoleum floor, I wonder if Danny is satisfied to see that I'm willing to fight for him. He seems to appreciate concrete shows of affection.

And then I'm pulled out of the fray by sturdy hands on my hips. "This isn't going to happen today, so just cool down, guys." It's Brody, five minutes too late.

"I'm gonna fuckin' sue you, asshole." Jared the fry cook points at me with one hand and cups his jaw with the other, pissed off as hell. He struggles to his feet, and though dazed, continues to rant. "That worm ain't got no business being back here. It says 'Employees Only' on the damn sign. And he fuckin' threw himself at me when I was just talking to my boyfriend."

"He's not your friggin' boyfriend." I stand up and shake out my limbs, one by one, but I'm too numb from the adrenaline rush to detect any pain.

"Perky, take a deep breath, man." Brody's already working his magic with soothing words. I feel the calm creep over me. "We need to get out of here, Danny. You coming?"

"I can't leave work. I'll get fired." Danny's voice is high-pitched and squeaky. I recognize the guilty tone. And his eyes are glued to the floor. He's making a choice, and it's not us. The thing with the three of us is over before it even got started.

It hurts too much to see and hear him like that, so I turn and walk out of the swinging door that I should never have come through in the first place.

IT'S ONE of the hardest things I've ever had to do to calm down after what happened in the restaurant, and I'm not talking about the physical fight with the loser fry cook who doesn't know the difference between snakes and worms. Danny's rejection is what has me bent out of shape.

Brody and I sit in his Jeep and try to chill out, but my anger doesn't fully subside until he puts his palm on my knee. When I feel the weight of his hand, I remember to do what he always tells me to do. I take a deep breath.

"What the fuck's he thinking?" I want so much to cover Brody's hand with my own and then to spend ten minutes staring at the perfect sight of my brown skin on top of his white skin. But I keep my hands folded in my lap.

"Maybe he isn't thinking, Henry."

"What's that supposed to mean?"

"What if he's just *reacting* to fear? You know, maybe he's looking for a sure thing—somebody who will stick with him so he won't have to be alone—and he doesn't think we're it."

"A 'sure thing,' as in a solid relationship?" I ask, but quickly slip into sarcasm. "You're saying the guy who beats him silly is a sure thing?"

Brody nods. "I think *he* sees it that way. Jared wants him and doesn't seem to be going anywhere. Just like with that kid, Sam, who cheated on him, right and left. Remember how Danny kept going back to him? And Ronnie the druggy? Danny stuck with him until he got tossed into jail."

Brody has a point. Still I argue, "But *we* can offer him more."

"Did we, though?" he asks. Score another point for Brody. "Don't you think we acted wishy-washy about being together?"

"I guess he'd need some faith that we're really in this thing— this relationship—with him. Danny would have to buy that we're gonna give it a serious shot," I say, thinking out loud.

"That's how I see it." Brody nods and squeezes my knee. "And we have to give him some time to believe in us."

"But I don't want him to be with that asshole, Jared."

"Henry, all we can do is prove to him that being with us is better."

I turn to the side in my seat, study Brody's expression, and note how he keeps on saying things that make sense. Then I really look at Brody. He must not have had time to spike up his freakish white-blond hair before he came to the restaurant to save us, because it droops over his forehead and makes him look like a little kid. He's also wearing baggy black basketball shorts and an even baggier red Just Do It T-shirt that make him look scrawny and young too.

"What happened there?" I point to his right knee, which is covered in a loose crisscross of bandages that barely cover the bloody mess underneath. His right elbow is in the same condition.

"The stairs at city hall had a slight disagreement with my mountain bike. That's all."

"Judging from your hair, you were smart enough to wear your helmet. Right?" I ask hopefully, because Brody too often "forgets" to wear it.

I can tell from Brody's shrug that it's wishful thinking on my part. "Are you saying my hair is flat?" he asks, pretending to be insulted, but I know it's just distraction.

"You've gotta be more careful, dude." Lectures don't work on plenty of people, and Brody is one of them. But I take a chance. I stick my hand on top of his, like I've been wanting to do since we got into the Jeep, and though I'm freaking out, I don't jerk it back when he turns his hand up and grasps mine. "Bro, I don't want to have to visit you in the hospital. You know?" I keep it short so he doesn't tune me out.

Brody's eyes—I'm almost certain they're the exact same threatening gray as the sky on the night of the storm at Branton Beach— are laser focused on me. And not in the "no worries, dude, I've got this" way I'm used to. He looks bewildered, like I just pulled the rug out from beneath his feet.

"I guess I'll wear my helmet next time," he replies in a soft voice.

Brody's notebook

SUNDAY, SEPTEMBER 28
> ~~A Voice Crying Out in the Hallways~~
> *Who ever said that all diaries require titles? There's no law.*
> *Sunday sucked.*

Henry was off all day doing the dutiful-son, church-and-dinner thing, as if he has any choice in the matter. Poor kid barely gets his head above water long enough to take a breath on Sundays. And I got a short text from Danny saying that he'd let me know if/when he needed a ride to school again, which was his nonconfrontational way of telling me, "The three of us are toast, as both lovers and friends, so keep your distance, dude." And since Mom and Dad are in Salem kicking off fall, "Little Brody" hung around the house by himself all day, fighting depression, which is not a good look for me. Saturday night's corn maze and sleepover that I'd been living for didn't happen, and I also knew it was the least of my worries. Danny had bailed out of our threelationship so he could be with a guy who physically abuses him. And it looked permanent. Or until Jared killed Danny. *Dang.*

By four in the afternoon, I'd had enough of myself and my compulsive thinking, so I made the decision that it would be a good opportunity to see how fast I could get to the Slippery Stone Outlet Mall in Raymond, and I got in the Jeep. My record is twenty-two minutes, but I was feeling confident that I could shave down my time by at least sixty seconds if I hit seventy on the back road by the dump. But I ended up canning that idea. Once I buckled into the driver's seat, I decided it would be a better idea to stalk Danny.

IT COULD HAPPEN

I sat outside his apartment building for two hours. All I spied was the same pair of old men with swollen bellies I'd seen last time I stalked Danny. They sat together on the front steps, simultaneously increasing their chances of getting liver disease *and* lung cancer. I got the added treat of witnessing a set of teenage moms and their cranky two-year-olds park baby strollers at the building's front door, exchange a couple of unfriendly words with the old men, and head inside to eat their bagged fast-food dinners.

There was no Danny, the missing gay-threesome member. And no Jared, the violent fry cook. In fact I got no results from two hours of covert observation. I'm a failure as a stalker.

Brody's notebook

MONDAY, SEPTEMBER 29
I had no clue what to expect of Henry when I picked him up this morning, but I really should have predicted it. He was in typical Henry passive-aggressive mode—fury and frustration thinly veiled by false bravado.

We sat silently in the Jeep until we stopped at the railroad crossing on Smith Street, where Henry burst out with "So, no words of comfort for me today, Decker? No 'he'll be back once we prove we're the better choice'?" He looked at me with narrowed eyes, like *I'd* chased Danny away with a stick.

My solution to this problem was to do a nine-second zero-to-sixty and keep up the speed the rest of the way down Smith Street. "I told you before—we've got to show him we're a better option!" I'm not sure why, but I shouted that. My consolation was lame, but it was also all I could come up with on the fly. I didn't glance at him when I spoke. Instead I focused on the road.

Henry responded with, "I'd say we're gonna need an Easy button to get that done."

I don't think this totally dysfunctional thing Henry and I are now sharing is going to be enough to entice Danny back into our arms.

IT BUGS me when Henry doesn't eat probably as much as it bothers him when I don't eat. Lunch today wasn't time to fill our faces. It was just more opportunity to stare at each other awkwardly.

"You've got to eat, dude. We have cross country after school, and your body needs fuel. Right?" I brought up the subject as gently as possible.

"I'll eat when you do." Henry can be so obstinate.

The problem was, my stomach was in spew-up mode. I knew that anything I put down was going to make its big encore in the boys' room toilet. "Whatever." I sounded like Danny, who incidentally hadn't made an appearance in the cafeteria. I figured he was probably upstairs in the art-department teachers' lounge, eating with the eclectic crowd that suits him far better than we do.

At cross-country practice, Henry was sluggish and unmotivated—a perfect match for me. Lionel sailed past us at mile three. His cocky smirk nearly gave me the burst of energy necessary to chase after him so I could tackle his ass. But I settled for shaking my head, said, "What a jerk," and plodded along beside my sullen companion.

Henry and I are stuck in limbo. Are we still together? Do we even want to be, without Danny? Is Danny gone for good?

Any way you slice it, you come up with purgatory.

Glad I have *A Voice Crying Out in the Hallway* my notebook in which to confide all my misery.

Free Verse Poetry by Danny D

"Secure"
everything aching joins into one,
an opaque cloud blocking the sun

IT COULD HAPPEN

I must walk through this storm

alone, like a martyr at death
guilty that I stole their breath
afraid as a child in the night
injured, the loser of a fight
jealous, like the one in last place
lost as a call with no trace

the only shelter I can see
is in this false security

Henry: My life

FIRST WAGNER surges past me, and then the top three runners on
the Wilson Brown Bears Cross-Country Team go by me, one by one.
Each time I get passed feels like a stab in the gut. But when No-neck
Nelson awkwardly lopes by, I know I'm up a creek.

"You can do this, Perky." Brody's not even wearing running
shoes, but he breaks out of the small crowd at the top of Linden Hill to
run beside me. And then he's with me—baggy cargo-pocket fatigues
and work boots with a loose button-down shirt flying behind him, and
even wearing his backpack—racing along, offering encouragement.

"Pick up the pace now. Focus on getting past just Nelson for
starters. You're so much faster than him it's not even funny."

Brody doesn't look at me, but he keeps on rambling words of
inspiration until I pass Nelson. Then he retreats back into the scattered
group of spectators and calls out a final bit of advice. "Keep it up,
Henry. You've got this!"

But I don't "got it" at all. I run into the finish with my tail
between my legs and end up in fifth place.

Dad is in my face before I can blink.

"What on earth do you call *that*?" He grabs my shirt by the
Golden Eagle emblem on the front. "You call that an effort?"

I look around for Brody. I'm not sure why. It's not like he can save me from my dad. All I can see are teammates crossing the line and their parents and other students congratulating them.

"Look at me, son," Dad barks, and then he shakes me to make sure he has my full attention. "You think you're going to get into a Division One track school with a performance like *this*?" He jabs his watch with a pointed finger.

The people around us can't miss that Dad is basically exploding all over me in an ugly show of public parental frustration. It's like he thinks I ran slowly to hurt him.

"This is unacceptable." Again he looks at his watch. "I'm speechless."

As I again look around for Brody, I sincerely wish Dad *actually could be* speechless.

"Have you been taking lessons on how to get slower? Have you?" He won't let up.

Finally I see Brody come through the crowd. I think he heard my father's last insult, as he steps up to my side in an act of solidarity.

"And this pothead loser"—he gestures toward Brody with his elbow—"is most certainly the one who's teaching you how to run at the pace of a damned turtle."

We now have the attention of the entire crowd. Coach Wentworth stands behind Dad, looking seriously disturbed. He places his hand on Dad's shoulder and says, "Mr. Perkins, with all due respect, this is just one race. Henry's a little bit off his game today. I'm sure he'll perform much better next time."

Dad turns around and glares at Coach, who shakes his head in mute frustration but steps back.

"I'm seriously considering sending you off for a postgrad year at Northrop Sports Academy. Maybe there you'll be able to concentrate on the important things in life, like running faster, rather than wasting your time hanging around with boys who are never going to amount to anything." The crowd's attention shifts to Brody. He looks down at the grass.

IT COULD HAPPEN

I can't help it. I make one of those lame choking noises. I want to cry because everything is so fucked-up in my life, but I can't. So the messed-up, strangled sound just pops out from deep in my throat. Even Lionel Wagner cringes, none too eager to see an eighteen-year-old guy cry ten feet past the finish line of a stupid cross-country race. Brody leans against me, and we stand shoulder to shoulder and wait for what comes next.

Dad storms off—finally speechless—but before I have a chance to breathe a sigh of relief, Mom steps up and shepherds me a few yards away from Brody.

"Kneel down," she says in all seriousness and then drops to her knees on the grass despite the fact she's wearing a skirt. "Get on your knees and pray with me, Henry."

I look back at Brody, and his face is pale. He shakes his head slowly, but obedient as always, I get down on my knees in the grass beside Mom. The shocked stare of the crowd heats all of my exposed skin.

"Lord Jesus, we thank You for all of the blessings You have bestowed upon us. We ask that You hear our humble prayer," she begins, her head bowed and her eyes closed. "Please help our son to succeed, dear Jesus."

I don't bow my head or close my eyes. But I *do* pray. Silently. *Oh God. Public prayer. Please, no.*

"Let's do this at home, Mom," I manage to utter.

Apparently God hears my desperate plea and passes it on to my mother. She rises to her feet, as I do, takes me by the hand, and leads me to the family minivan. I don't look back at Brody. There's no point. Dad is waiting in the driver's seat. He refuses to look at me when I slide open the door and climb in back.

This afternoon was the crowning glory on a week from hell.

Brody's notebook

SUNDAY, OCTOBER 5
Adventures in Learning the Hard Way

On a night when Danny, Henry, and I should have been together racing around the Haunted Corn Maze at the Beans and More Beans Farm or eating pizza at the Italian Pie Joint, I was skateboarding along the metal railing of Scenic Bridge in Plimpton, trying not to look down at the rocky stream below.

I love the electrified feeling I get in my toes when my body knows enough to be scared shitless and my brain refuses to pay attention. I felt a little guilty about being so reckless, but in my defense, I technically had only told Henry I'd wear my helmet when I was *mountain biking.*

I needed to get that miserable scene at the cross-country meet with Henry and his obsessive parents out of my head, and since Henry was grounded and Danny was missing in action, I was the only one left to take care of the big job of distracting myself. I remember thinking, if I fall from this railing into the stream, it's very possible I won't get up. And I'm okay with that. But I focused my brain on not falling and made it back down to the wooden bridge in one piece. Over the course of the night, I didn't die, but I managed to rip off all my scabs from my adventures at City Hall.

Every time I got back on the ground, I again saw Henry standing in front of his father and on his knees beside his mother... just taking it.

He stood there and knelt there and took their shit.

To make the vision go away, my skateboard and I had to keep on getting up on that railing to see how far I could push it.

My plan for the immediate future—the next few days at a minimum—is to skip cross-country practice, which is one of the perks of not being an official team member.

There's only so much punishment a guy can take.

CHAPTER 6
BACK IN THE SADDLE

Brody's notebook

WEDNESDAY, OCTOBER 8
~~*The Story of Our Lives*~~

I came home right after school today—my third day in a row of skipping cross-country practice—with plans to crash on my bed and finally lose the battle with my tears, seeing as my friendship and romance with Henry and Danny were self-destructing in front of my very eyes. But just before I turned into the driveway, I saw Danny standing by our mailbox.

So I pulled over close enough for him to hear me say, "Get in and buckle up."

He did as I told him without argument, and as soon as I heard the click, I headed back toward the main road and put my plans to cry on my bed on hold.

"I suppose you think I screwed things up with Henry and you, right?" Danny asked in a tone that suggested he didn't give a shit what I thought.

"I think Jared's an asshole. Does that answer your question?" I replied, and I wasn't sweet about it either.

Danny shrugged but persisted. "And Henry can't be exactly pleased with me, I assume."

What he said was true, but I offered no confirmation. What was I supposed to say? "Yeah. Henry's one straw shy of a basket case and you nearly got me tossed off a bridge railing into a river. We're in very bad shape. Are you happy?"

"I couldn't let go of him." Danny was in full confession mode, and I knew immediately he was talking about Jared. "I just hate being alone."

Danny may hate being alone, but I hated his words. And I'm only human. I couldn't make myself look at him. But I *could* spit out a sarcastic comment. "So you decided to stick it out with a guy who hits you?" To sum it up, I was disgusted and jealous, and a big part of me was just plain tired. "Smart choice, Danny."

"I only got back with Jared for a few days," he claimed, and I didn't want to care.

And I didn't want to beg him to tell me what he was talking about, but I did. "What are you saying? Tell me."

"I dumped Jared last weekend," he offered. His gaze was on my face as he sized me up.

I refused to let him analyze me so easily and covered my relieved smile by glancing sideways out the window. By the end of freshman year, I knew when it was time to sit back and shut up with Danny. It was one of those times, so that's what I did.

"I steered clear of Jared all this week at work too, so it's a done deal with him, I guess."

I nodded again, like none of what he was saying was a big deal, but my heart started to pound with hope.

"Well, that's all I wanted to say, so I guess you can dump me off here," Danny finished. His expression was blank and his voice flat. He never gives away more than he has to.

"I'm not going to leave you in the middle of freaking nowhere."

"I'd deserve it," he said beneath his breath. Danny's not the kind of guy to say he's sorry, but that was what I'd call an admission of guilt.

"Let's go get some food?" I heard myself suggest.

When I looked over at him, he shrugged and nodded—a classic example of Danny being Danny.

IT COULD HAPPEN

We went to Wendy's drive-thru. I got us a couple orders of french fries and a large chocolate Frosty to share, and we sat in the Jeep in the back of the parking lot to eat. It was quiet for a long time.

Danny was the one who broke the silence. "It was freaking me out to think I was gonna leave a sure bet with Jared to be in some fucked-up, 'ain't never gonna happen' threesome that we supposedly had going."

I'd figured as much. I wanted to reach into his mouth and pull the next ten sentences out of his throat, but instead I played it cool and chomped on a small stack of fries. "And?"

"And I'm gonna *officially* tell Jared to take a permanent hike," he answered and looked straight at me. "Tonight."

Danny's light eyes were outlined with extra heavy-duty black guyliner, making it hard to read his expression, so I had to go by what he told me. Again I nodded, the picture of cool, even though I thought he had already said it was over with Jared before.

"Will you tell Henry what I just told you and see if he's still up for doing this threesome thing?" Danny asked. He looked so nervous that I wanted to hug him, but again, I held back.

"Yeah… I'll tell him." I'm soft when it comes to Henry and Danny, though, and I quickly decided not to make him suffer too much. I mumbled something like, "He'll probably be into it," and I hoped I wasn't lying. Having been seriously hurt by Danny's unexpected exit, Henry wasn't exactly the same as before.

"Thanks, Brody." I got one of those halfhearted Danny smirks, and I immediately felt better.

"Can you… you know, handle things with Jared? Like if he gets mad when you tell him it's over?" It was time to look at the business end of our venture, and Danny's safety was most important.

"I already went to my boss and asked to be put on separate shifts from Jared. And I'll tell him that we're toast in public, so he can't kick the shit outta me."

I said, "That works." But I couldn't stop myself from shuddering.

"And Brody, I got no clue what happens next in a threesome, but I guess I'm gonna give it a shot, you know, as long as Henry's still into it." It was interesting to see Danny so far out of his comfort zone. But then he changed from looking uncomfortable to worried. And I knew for sure he'd missed us, even if he didn't say it. I knew because I'd missed us too.

"Stop worrying, Danny-boy."

Danny nodded, and suddenly I wanted him to get the hell out of my Jeep. I wanted to quit while I was ahead. Without saying anything else, I drove pretty fast in the direction of Danny's apartment. He was back on the same page as me as far as us trying to get something going with the three of us. If Henry still wanted to do it, maybe things would work out. But I needed to get him the hell out of my Jeep before something went wrong.

I pulled over on the street in front of Danny's building. He looked relieved to be quitting while he was ahead too.

"Let me know if you need help with Jared. And I'll pick you up in the morning for school. Okay?" I said as he got out of the Jeep. "Don't worry. I'll talk to Henry tonight."

"K." Danny nodded, and he blinked once, like he was surprised that it had been so simple to win me back. Then he turned around and walked toward the apartment building without saying goodbye.

Henry: My life

I'M STILL grounded, but Brody doesn't seem to give a crap.

"Just tell them you need to go to the store to pick up a piece of poster board for a project that's due tomorrow."

"They aren't going to buy that. They know I'd never save a project for the last minute," I argue. Mom and Dad weren't born yesterday.

"Say your ankle is a little bit sore, and you want to go pick up an ACE bandage for practice tomorrow."

"That might work," I say. Dad would let me do anything if it meant I'd run faster. "Okay. I'll ask him. Hang on." I put my phone on the bed and run down the hall.

"Hey, Dad." I'm awkward as shit, but not because I'm lying. I'm *always* lying to him. I'm awkward with my father because I feel like such a disappointment. "I was thinking that maybe my times have been slow because my right ankle feels a little shaky."

He literally drops the remote onto the floor. "You mean your ankle feels *weak?*"

"Maybe a little."

"We need to get you to the doctor, then."

"I was thinking that maybe I'd pick up an ACE bandage at the pharmacy tonight, if you'd let me use the minivan. And if it helps in practice tomorrow, maybe we can talk about picking up some different running shoes. Ones with a little more support."

Dad's eyes light up. "So maybe you ran slowly at the last meet because you tweaked your ankle…. Now *that* makes sense." He reaches into his pocket and hands me the keys and some cash. "Go to the sports shop, rather than a pharmacy. Take your time and look over all the elastic bandages… and be sure to ask an employee which kind is best."

"I will, Dad." I run back down the hall to my room. "I'll meet you at the Sports Center at the shopping plaza, Brody. I'm gonna have to actually come home with an ACE bandage."

BRODY IS waiting for me when I get to the shopping plaza downtown. He's not waiting patiently, though. He's pacing back and forth in front of his Jeep, and he runs to the minivan and hops in as soon as I park.

"We need to talk," he says, out of breath.

"I figured as much," I reply. I'm still pissed off that Brody skipped practice all week, but I don't say anything about it.

"I saw Danny today after school."

"You saw him?" I echo.

"I talked to him too."

I want to play it cool, but I can't. "What did he say?"

"He wants to try things with us again."

I usually know exactly how I feel, but not then. Part of me is thrilled, another part relieved, but the rest of me is the problem. The rest of me is as mad as hell at Danny for dumping us… and maybe a little bit scared for reasons I'd rather not dwell on.

"He asked me to tell you that it's over with Jared. And that he wants to be with us instead." Brody's eyes are huge, probably as wide as I've ever seen them.

"Come on. Let's go into the store. I have to buy an ACE bandage." I get out of the minivan, and Brody sits there for a second, but then he comes after me.

When we get into the store, Brody gives me a little more detail about his conversation with Danny. "He told me he was afraid of leaving what he was *sure* he had with Jared for something experimental with us."

I nod. "I get that."

"And that he's going to tell Jared it's completely over with them."

"I should fucking hope so."

Brody smiles and takes a hold of my wrist. "He's back, Henry. Danny came back."

I have to swallow hard not to make one of those choking noises I'm getting kind of famous for. Frankly I'm freaking out.

Brody slips his hand down so he's holding mine. It feels so fuckin' good. For a second I forget to look around and make sure no one is watching, and I latch on to him like a little kid to his mother before they cross a busy street. "Okay. Let's go for it."

Brody breaks into the biggest grin I've ever seen. "Yes! I'll tell Danny. And do you think you can go out Saturday night? We can do the whole corn-maze and sleepover thing that we were supposed to do last weekend."

"I'll ask my parents."

"I'll cross my fingers and my toes, Perky."

I suddenly realize that we're standing in front of the display of sports injury bandages, holding hands, and I pull mine back. "Dad will probably say yes if I can tell him I shaved off time in practice tomorrow."

Brody folds his arms over his chest and looks at the floor. "Yeah… uh, sorry I've missed a few practices."

"Will you be at practice tomorrow?"

"I wouldn't miss it. We have work to do."

The worst week in the history of my high school career ends on a decent note.

Henry: My life

BRODY'S SATURDAY-NIGHT plans for the three of us are miraculously back on. They're just somewhat delayed. And although I thought my father was going to tell me I couldn't go, he surprised me by saying he thought I needed to "de-stress." That was a major change in tune, but of course, I didn't argue. Talk about gifts from God. That was surely one.

Brody picks me up just before five. Of course Mom and Dad are staring out the front door as I get into the Jeep. Their expressions are worried, as though I'm descending into the fires of hell. I *think* exactly what Danny would say—"whatever." I'm just happy I'm free for the night and, even more than that, I'm psyched that I'm gonna see Danny. It's been a while.

We go straight over to Danny's building, and he's waiting on the sidewalk, dressed all in black. No surprise. Crazy thing is, when I see him standing there in his black leggings and tunic thingy, I get a hard-on. That has never happened to me before—scratch that—a hard-on has happened to me before, but not as a response to merely *seeing* Danny standing beside the road.

How does my dick know we're on a date?

Danny climbs into the Jeep, and I slide into the back. Suddenly it's awkward as hell. I'm one of the two jilted boyfriends here, and I feel the sting of it, not to mention the fear that it's gonna happen again.

Before Danny is settled in the Jeep, Brody turns back toward me and murmurs, "Take a leap of faith, Perky."

And shit, things didn't go too smoothly last week when we were each heading in our own separate directions, so I reply, "I'm gonna try."

Brody pauses before he pulls his Jeep onto the street, and Danny turns in his seat, looks from me to Brody, and says, "I screwed up big-time with you guys."

And that's all. Danny offers no "I'm sorry. Please forgive me." But it works.

"Not *too much* harm done," Brody jokes, and although that isn't nearly enough discussion on the topic, none of us wants to have any more. We aren't big talkers, I guess. Brody pulls onto the street, and just like that, we're on our first real date.

The Jeep ride is completely silent until Brody finally says, "I thought we'd go to PJ's Pub for dinner. You guys cool with that?"

I'm always hungry, but food is the last thing on my mind. I just spent too long convinced that one of my best friends was lost to me forever and I was busy screwing everything up with my other best friend like it was my job. *Everything* was fucked-up. Over the past couple weeks, it became clear to each of us that we're either all in or all out.

It's a threesome, or we're done.

"Toast," as Danny says.

And now I'm with *both* of them. I'm off the clock with regard to my parents, and I'm pretty sure I'm planning to throw caution to the wind.

"I don't give a shit where we eat," I reply as I realize that Brody is waiting for an answer.

Danny chimes in with "PJ's Pub is cool. I love their mango smoothies." He seems nervous, but I guess it makes sense. The kid blew us off so he could decide whether or not he was into Jared, the fuckin' elderly fry cook. And it hurt like hell to wait, but he made his choice. Now he's here with us.

A line of sweat rises on my upper lip.

Brody turns toward me and Danny and smiles. It's hot as hell. His smile erases all of the lingering bad shit in my head.

ONCE WE arrive at the restaurant, a noticeable change comes over Brody. All of a sudden, he's a dude on a date, acting polite and gentlemanly. It turns me on, even though I'm not sure if it's appropriate to sport a raging erection in a nice restaurant.

"Dinner's on me, you guys," he announces once we're seated in a corner booth. We sit just like we used to do in the cafeteria before our relationship went to hell—me across from Brody and Danny. I wish it were darker because I really want to take both of their hands in mine on top of the table, but we can't do that in the light of day. Plus I've never made a move like that, and one of us might have a heart attack from the shock.

I'm not sure where I get the balls, but I hook my feet with theirs beneath the table. Brody and Danny's eyes pop open wide when they realize we're rubbing our feet together. Maybe their dicks won't let them forget that tonight is different from all the other nights either.

"What do you want to eat?" Brody asks, a little breathless.

Danny answers in a similarly raspy voice. "I'm in a pasta mood."

So I say, "I'm in the mood for pasta too."

Brody smiles. "Then it's noodles all around."

And after we order, it's time to talk.

"You know how I was missing in action?" Danny looks overwhelmed. "Well, I'm sorry. Like I said before, I screwed up."

I think Brody and I are both surprised that Danny actually apologized.

"We're here now, so it worked out fine." Brody always knows what to say when I don't, which is most of the time.

Danny offers more in the way of explanation, although sorry was enough for me. "It was hard for me to believe that this thing with us could be real."

"We're sitting here together playing footsie. I'd say it's real." I'm not always smooth, but I can be honest.

"Thanks for the second chance."

Danny's light eyes are so pretty—maybe even more so than usual right now, because he's a little bit scared and a lot hopeful and he seems genuinely happy to be here. "Not a problem," I reply.

"So what comes next? How do we morph into whatever it is the three of us are trying to become?" Danny wants to know what's up, and I don't have any answers. I just know what I want, and they're sitting across from me.

Again Decker steps in to save my ass. "I think we just be together and like it. *And* let ourselves like *each other* more than we think we should." He toes off a boat shoe and curls his foot around my ankle.

Other than what's going on with our feet under the table, we eat dinner like three regular guys. It's not so different from when we were just friends, but it's like we've got a secret.

REAL LIFE finds its way into the corn maze. We arrive at the Beans and More Beans Farm only to see Lionel, Jamie, and a whole crowd of the athletes from the Jocks"R"Us lunch table milling around like they own the place and all the beans that grow there. I want to groan, but I don't. My job is to look out for Brody and Danny and to make sure our first real date isn't a shit show, like it easily could be.

"Look, it's the sandwich cookie. They're on a date." Lionel never knows when to shut his mouth. But still he hits the nail on the friggin' head.

I'm not in the mood for it. I want to relax and let loose and enjoy this night. So naturally I overreact. "What the fuck do you care, Wagner? Unless you're jealous." I grab my crotch. "You want some of this?"

Wagner's in my face before I can take another breath, but then Brody appears on my other side, leans in toward me so our shoulders are pressed together, and speaks up. "Look, Wagner, we're here for the same reason you are—to blow off a little steam. So why don't you and your gang head into the maze? I promise, you won't see us again."

"You sure you don't wanna *blow* something else?" he asks Brody with a wink and a grin, and I want to slug the smile right off his face.

80

But I keep my clenched fists at my sides, and my restraint pays off. Lionel and his crew head into the maze without any more bullshit.

We wait awhile to give them time to get well ahead of us, and then Brody, Danny, and I set off into the maze. I want it to be romantic, but there are so many little kids running around that the most it can be is fun. So we let it be that.

I want to hold my boyfriends' hands, but it's a stupid urge that can only bring us trouble, so instead, we walk side by side and stay as close as we can. I'm happy to brush shoulders with Danny, who acts like he's bored with mazes even if he isn't, and Brody, who has put all of his eggs in our strange basket.

As we explore the maze, and weigh and measure which way to go, we're again a team. It reminds me of freshman year, when we figured out how to play badminton in gym class.

What's to come next, at Brody's house, is anyone's guess. But soon it's time to move on. It's time for us to be alone together.

My dick likes the idea. The rest of me is scared shitless.

Free verse poetry by Danny D

"Hiding Spots"
When we stop hiding in our favorite spots,
Behind words and anguish and distractions,
Will we find a path to contentment?
To happy days where beds of roses line easy streets?
Or will we fly so high, only to tumble to the ground,
Where bad news and hard luck drive us to yearn
For the sweet hiding spots of yesterday?

Brody's notebook

SUNDAY, OCTOBER 12
    ~~Three Guys' Tales~~ *(nope—sounds too much like porn)*

I like the word epic. *It's more timeless than* stellar. *And it comes closer to describing something monumental than the overused* awesome. *Saturday night was epic.*

Considering the circumstances, dinner wasn't as awkward as expected. The corn maze was fun too. But when we got back to my place, we found out who we were. We found out what *us* was. At first it was awkward. What would you expect? We're three guys, all wanting something we're scared to want and even more scared to get—something that would make us more different than we already are at school and could possibly inspire our families to turn their backs on us. But still we headed upstairs to my suite, and once there, we opened ourselves up to one another.

"Opening up" was a new look for us. Danny didn't say "whatever" even once. Henry didn't get bent out of shape. I didn't take off running. Opening up was a giant first step, but we all wanted to figure out if we could have something together. Being honest was critical.

When we got to my third-floor suite, I felt like it was my job to make Danny and Henry feel comfortable. So I told them to sit down, and I pointed to my sofa. Danny planted his butt on the couch, but Henry went straight to the bed.

"I want to sit *here*," Henry told us. He was bold about it, which could have been false bravado. But he went ahead and made himself comfortable on my bed, and I was cool with it. Sitting on the middle of my California king, Henry really *looked* like a king.

A big part of me wanted to exit stage left and head downstairs to grab a bottle of vodka from my parents' liquor cabinet. Being drunk would soften the situation. It would make things easier for all of us, because if we were drunk, we wouldn't have to take full responsibility for what we said and did. But Henry and I don't drink at all, and Danny only parties when he's with one of his "legal to buy booze" boyfriends. So instead of getting the vodka, I went to the small refrigerator at my wet bar, and grabbed three cans of all-natural soda. I brought them to the night table, and we all met on the bed. Danny and I found places to sit up by the headboard on either side of King Henry. We concentrated on our cans of black cherry soda like they were the last things on earth we'd ever drink.

"This is fucked-up," Danny said, and even though I agreed, I shook my head as if he were wrong.

But Henry spoke up. "Not so much," he said, and then he pulled off his T-shirt. Typically I'm the one to use distraction to my benefit, so I've got to give Henry credit for his brilliant move. All Danny and I could do was gawk at him, even though we'd seen Henry half-naked a hundred times before. Sure, he was beautiful—all cut muscles and smooth brown skin—but right then it was better because he was beautiful *and* he was sort of ours.

"Take your shirts off too," he said, but he managed to sound casual about it. More points to him. Danny and I ripped our shirts over our heads, but knowing we were nothing but skin and bones compared to Henry, we crossed our arms over our chests.

Henry didn't seem to think our bodies were anything less than perfect, though. He said something like, "Oh yeah," when he saw us shirtless and within his reach. Then he lay back down in the middle of my bed and patted the spots on either side of him. "Come lie down with me, you guys."

Danny was nervous. He crawled to the inside of the bed, between Henry and the wall, but he didn't cozy up to Henry. Then he stuck his back against the wall and stared at me to see what I would do. I went to Henry's other side and made myself lie down beside him, fully aware that I was no doubt taking a risk. Henry reached over and took my hand in his, which was almost more than I could take. To feel his big, warm hand holding on to mine and know that he was there, not just as my best friend, but also as someone who wanted to share *more* with me, kind of blew my mind.

When Danny saw our clasped hands, it was like a huge magnet pulled him to us. He stretched out on the other side of Henry, but he was still super nervous—which didn't make sense. He's the only one of us who has any experience in the sexual arena. Maybe it's different for Danny because it will actually *mean something* to him to be with us. When he was with other guys, he was just trying to please them. When Henry put an arm around his shoulder and drew him in, Danny finally let go and threw his arm over Henry's chest. His hand came to rest on my wrist.

The feeling of being that close to these guys was bigger than big—mind-blowingly huge—which is the only way to describe the way we were stretching the limits of our friendship. What we were doing was dangerous and thrilling and scary as hell.

The three of us had crossed into virgin territory, pretty much literally. I was lying beside my closest friend, both of us were unsure of what we were doing, and our other best friend's arm was draped across us.

And we'd never before been much closer than a fist bump.

Henry let out a loud sigh, and though it was a release of anxiety, he was definitely not relaxed. Danny was uptight too. When he heard Henry sigh, he tightened his hold on my wrist. We were all on edge, but I knew we'd broken through the first barrier.

"This isn't just friendship between us. It can't be." Henry put my thoughts into words. Danny nodded too.

And then we held one another. I have no clue how long we stayed stuck together that way. After making the monumental move to get close, I think we were all afraid to mess it up by shifting our bodies so much as an inch. After what seemed like an hour, I suggested we get ready for bed.

Henry and Danny had brought backpacks that they'd dropped by the door when they came into my suite. They dragged themselves from my bed, got their bags, and took turns in the bathroom. Then I did the same. When I got back to the bed, Danny and Henry were under the covers, and Danny's head rested on Henry's chest. For some reason the sight made me stop in my tracks and stare. I'm pretty sure I smiled too. It was about the sweetest thing I'd ever seen.

When I was done memorizing the vision, I turned off the light on my night table and got into bed, but I didn't place my head on Henry's chest like Danny had. Before I did anything like that again,

I had something to say. "I'm not going to get physically close to you guys if this is just a thing for one night."

I was honest with them, and it was their turn to make me believe it was real.

Danny sniffed loudly enough for me to hear. Although I knew trusting was hard for him—even harder than having a sexual relationship would be—I wasn't willing to relax my standards just because Danny was willing to get busy with us in the bed. This was going to be something real or it was going to be nothing at all. Maybe it *was* my house, but I had no problem hitting the road if it came to that.

I won't ever forget what Henry said next or how he said it. "I need this with you guys," he admitted with urgency. "The past few weeks sucked because I thought I lost the chance to get close to you two. But now, everything's different... and it's... so much better. I want to hold you both all night. But for me this thing isn't just about *tonight*."

Danny made a weird whimpering noise that somehow convinced me he wanted it to be more than a one-night stand too. So I turned on my side, put my head on Henry's shoulder, and placed my hand on his belly. Danny's hand was already waiting there, and we automatically laced our fingers together.

Once again we were quiet for a long time as we held one another. My thoughts were scattered just about everywhere—aware of both the risk and the opportunity waiting for us in that bed—as I tried my best to drink in the magnitude of our new bond.

"How can we ever go back to just being friends?" I once again asked what seemed to be the theme of the night. And then I answered my own question. "We *can't* go back." I knew for a fact that once I shared myself with those guys—touching their skin and memorizing how we fit together—it would be too late for us to ever be just friends again.

"Who said anything about going back?" And with those words, Danny climbed on top of Henry. Without letting go of my hand, he kissed Henry's lips—long and deep—and like in my dreams, I simply watched. But my toes tingled with the enormity of what I saw. Then Danny slid onto me, pressed his lips to mine, and opened his mouth. I heard a moan when our tongues came together and our nakedness touched. The little moan sounded like it came from miles away, but I knew *I* made that sound. I made it in the bed I've slept in every night since I was a kid, where I suddenly wasn't a kid anymore. And there was so much closeness between the three of us—and years of friendship—I hardly knew how to categorize it.

Danny stopped kissing me long enough to give Henry a chance to have his turn. Henry's kiss was firm and dry, where Danny's had been mushy and wet. I craved more of both kinds. When Henry lifted his lips from mine and we all looked at one another, it was like we made an unspoken decision to let go of everything we'd been holding on to so tightly for so long—maybe even for years. Like magic, we released all of it at once—our fears, our self-control, our restraint—and began to move together like we knew what we were doing.

Henry found my dick and I curled my hands around both Danny's and Henry's dicks. They were as hard and needy as I was. Danny sunk into the little hollow between us, and a frantic, sloppy and awesome make-out session ensued. All of our lips merged in a heated tangle of tongues. We were all breathless and I was pretty overwhelmed, but I think we were all sure of what we wanted. And I'd never felt so bonded with Henry and Danny in my mind, but at the same time so focused on my own body feeling good. It didn't take long until we were thrusting into one another's hands while Danny held us together in a tight hug. There was nothing sophisticated about it. It was a frenzied, chaotic mesh of bodies and feelings. Soon we burst with the intensity.

As my breathing slowed down, I knew that for me, things could never be the same. I wondered if Danny and Henry could go back to what we were before if they tried. But my head wasn't filled with worry anymore because I was so certain of how it had to be. Again flat on our backs, we lay in a row, breathed in unison, still sweating from the exertion. And since none of us could find the right words for how we'd changed since we climbed into my bed not too many minutes earlier, we gravitated toward Danny, who was between us. We wrapped our arms around him, put our hands on one another, and fell asleep.

CHAPTER 7
I'M WITH THEM

Free Verse Poetry by Danny D

We wear hard shells,
Smooth as polished marble,
A shatterproof cut diamond,
Cold and slippery, like ice on a sidewalk,
Harder to break than addiction.

But even hard shells crack.
The solid, stiff casing loosens and falls apart,
Folding in upon itself,
Exposing hidden softness.

Stripped of our shells,
Now porous as a yellow kitchen sponge,
As floppy as a puppy's ear,
Gentle and tender, like a mother's touch,
More vulnerable than sobriety.

Henry: My life

IN THE morning I wait for Brody to pick me up for school in the driveway instead of on the porch with my mother. I know she's hurt because usually early mornings are the time that Mom and I take a few minutes to chat about what we're doing that day and say a few prayers. She values these moments, and I used to value them too, but lately I've been holding back so much from her. It has become an effort to pretend I'm being open when I'm really just trying not to lie to her face.

I don't want my mom to see my expression when I first set eyes on Brody. Everything is different since Saturday night, and I'm not sure how I'm going to react when I see him. Before Brody drove us home on Sunday morning, we slipped right back into awkward mode. Who am I kidding? We slipped into awkward mode the second our eyes opened Sunday morning to the sight of one another—naked and afraid, just like those awkward survivalists on the Discovery Channel television show.

When his Jeep comes down the road, my heart pounds, and my mouth gets dry. Our eyes lock when the Jeep is *two* telephone poles away, and I can't look away. I don't want to look away.

My brain screams, "Oh shit. He's so hot!" Brody has never looked better to me. "See ya tonight, Mom," I say without turning to look at her.

When the Jeep stops in the driveway, I hop in and find myself unable to look at Brody, after I stared at him all the way down the street. I know exactly what I'd see if I were to look—hopeful gray eyes, a straight nose that miraculously has never been broken despite the crazy risks he takes, and a wide smile. It's all framed by blond hair that's spiked-up but still soft, which I know from running my fingers through it on Saturday night. But instead of looking, I glance down at my sneakers and wait.

Brody always knows what to say. "I don't know about you, but I didn't sleep half as well last night as I did on Saturday night. Catch my drift?" He laughs.

It's the perfect thing to say. I blow out the breath I've been holding on to since the second I saw the Jeep and become me again. "I know what you mean." It's suddenly safe to look at him, and what I see is better than what I expected, because he looks at me like a boyfriend would.

"Let's go get Danny. I have something I want to show you guys."
Brody doesn't burn rubber when he pulls out of my driveway.

From a distance it looks like a ninja is standing on the sidewalk
in front of Danny's apartment building. He's wearing black leggings
and a snug, black, hooded sweatshirt with the hood up and drawn
tight. If I had to guess, I'd say he's hiding inside because he isn't sure
how to act with Brody and me after what we did together Saturday
night. I slide into the backseat so he can jump in, and while Brody
waits to hear the two seatbelts click, we don't speak.

"I'd kill for a cup of coffee," Danny finally says as he stares
straight ahead.

Brody is ready with a comeback. "Anything for you, Danny-
boy." He turns around in the building's parking lot and heads for the
Canteen Café.

Danny hooks up his iPhone to the aux cord and we listen to
indie music, which saves us from having to communicate. It feels like
a brief stay of execution, so it's hard to enjoy the tunes. Brody goes
to the drive-through and picks up Danny's coffee. Then he pulls into
a spot in the front of the lot.

"I went and did something yesterday. I want to show you guys."

And right there in the parking lot of the Canteen Café, Brody
slides onto his side, tugs on his jeans, and reaches back to push his
boxers down off of the cheek of his ass. And yeah, I like his body a
lot, but it's 7:00 a.m. on a Monday morning and there's a lot of traffic
around here.

The thing is, Brody's showing us his butt, and I can't exactly
not look. There on his perfectly shaped left ass cheek is a good-sized
tattoo of two hands with fingers pointing in opposite directions. The
ink is black, but the tattoo appears to be a purplish color because it's
red and irritated. "Read it," Brody demands.

We focus on the small words printed neatly above the pointing
hands.

"I'm with them," Danny reads the message slowly.

Brody cranes his neck to look at us, and grins widely. "Yeah.
That's what it says."

"You went and got a tattoo for *us*?" I ask.

Brody nods, and he looks proud, his butt still bare as the day he was born.

"Cool," Danny says. He has a few homemade tattoos of his own, so apparently they're on the same wavelength. Brody's gesture is appreciated by his Goth boyfriend.

"Whoa," I say.

"Don't worry, Henry. You don't have to get a tattoo to make me happy," Brody tells me as though he's read my mind. "I just wanted you guys to know that this is real for me."

Danny nods. "Good move, Brody." The concrete visual declaration of our threesome status seems to work for Danny. "I like it."

"What do *you* think of it, Henry?" Brody asks.

I swallow hard, both moved and shocked by what he did. A tattoo is permanent. It's not something that usually goes along with a romantic fling. "This is real."

"Yup, it's real. I can't wash it off," Brody confirms.

I meant that what the three of us are doing in our relationship is real, but I let Brody think I was talking about the tattoo. Decker finally tugs his boxers and jeans up over his ass, sits back down on the driver's seat with a small grimace, and looks from Danny to me. Danny leans across the center console and hugs Brody. "I'm psyched you did this. I'm gonna get the same one when I turn eighteen. Will you take me to the tattoo parlor where you got it?"

"Done deal." Brody is one with Danny.

"This is real," I say again, beneath my breath. I feel alone and very much on the outside.

Danny and Brody look at me.

"I can't get a tattoo," I tell them. "My folks would have my head."

Brody grins. "That's okay, Perky. We'll still let you hang around with us." He's trying to get me to smile too, but I can't. I want an "I'm With Them" tattoo more than I ever thought I would, and another tiny feeling of resentment toward my parents settles into the back of my mind.

I also want to touch my boyfriends, and Mom and Dad aren't there to stop me. So I reach out with both arms and put my hands on their shoulders. It feels right. "Thanks for getting yourself inked for us, Decker."

Brody covers my hand with his, and then Danny turns his face so his cheek rubs my hand.

I get little bumps all up and down my arms, and I find myself saying it one more time. "This is real."

Brody's notebook

FRIDAY, OCTOBER 17
~~Brody Speaks~~ uh, nope
~~A Journey to the Center of My Mind~~ and one more time, nope
Once again on Thursday night, after cross-country practice, I embraced my willingness to be a Peeping Tom. I needed to be certain that I'm Danny's one and only stalker, and that Jared the thug fry cook is ancient history.

Plus I was hungry. It was well past five o'clock, and I'd missed dinner with Mom and Dad. A guy needs to eat, even if I mostly eat vegetables.

So after I dropped Henry off at home, I drove straight to the Food Pyramid where Danny works most afternoons. And lo and freaking behold, who was sitting on the pretty yellow bench beside the restaurant's entrance, but Jared himself?

I didn't want to jump to conclusions—Jared could have been there to talk to the manager about creative fry-cooking techniques or to pick up his paycheck so he could buy booze for another underage guy. Just because his faded-denim-clad backside was resting casually on the dang bench didn't mean he was necessarily there to harass or attempt to steal my boyfriend. I parked the Jeep in a far corner of the lot and then turned all the way around in my seat and craned my neck to the extreme left so I could do my very best job of covert observation. And by that I mean stalking.

IT COULD HAPPEN

My efforts paid off quickly. I watched for only about five minutes, and then Danny came out of the restaurant. He looked younger and more innocent than usual, thanks to the fact that he's not allowed to wear black clothing to work. In fact, from the neck down, he resembled a slim Catholic schoolboy in a red polo shirt, snug khaki pants, and clean white running sneakers. From the neck up, his image still screamed *emo gay boy*! Merely having his shoulder-length hair pulled back into a ponytail couldn't completely alter the radical effect of his very-pierced personal style.

I admit that I tensed up when he walked straight over to Jared. I'm not sure why I felt sudden stress. Either I was worried that Jared was going to try to hurt Danny or I experienced a brewing jealousy that one of my guys was fraternizing with his ex.

But he didn't sit down beside Jared on the sunny yellow bench. Danny put his hands on his hips, he bent forward a little bit, and from what I could see at a distance, he lowered his eyebrows. Familiar with Danny's body language, I could safely assume that he and Jared were not going to have a conversation about which park they'd be going to after work to collect pretty fall leaves.

Jared immediately took a familiar defensive position, marked by the way he crossed his arms in front of his chest. And for the next five minutes, Danny tore him a new one. That was probably as clear to the diners who passed by as it was to me, Brody the Spy, who strained to peek at them from an obstructed view about eight cars away. When Danny was finished, he removed one hand from his hip, turned, and pointed to a shiny Kawasaki motorcycle that was parked by the street. I distinctly heard him demand, "Just go away."

Jared, still a cool customer, stood up, shrugged like he didn't care, and then skulked off toward his bike. Before he had time to rev it up and ride out of the parking lot, though, Danny turned toward my apparently not well hidden Jeep and walked straight over to me.

"Learn anything interesting?" he asked without any effort to hide his sarcasm. Then he sent me a glare that would have shattered the driver's side window, had I not already lowered it.

I immediately started to ramble because I was caught. "I… uh… I noticed that you… you had a little chat… with Jared."

"You noticed, did you?" Danny made it clear he wasn't buying my line.

"Yeah, I did." I swallowed hard and scrambled for a convenient means of distraction, but came up empty. "Did you have a productive discussion?"

"What do you think?" Danny answered my questions with more questions of his own, which couldn't be good.

I wiped the sweat off my forehead with the sleeve of my sweatshirt.

"Look, Brody. I told Jared last week that we were done. He just came by today to make sure I meant it," Danny explained.

"From what I could see, you… uh… you did," I replied.

"Damned straight, I did." Danny tugged on the elastic band that held back his hair, and when he pulled it out, the blue tips of his jet-black hair spilled over his shoulders. But his voice got soft and gentle when he said, "Dude, you gotta relax."

I shrugged and said, "I can try."

Then he offered me a little bit more honesty than I'm used to. "Listen, I'm willing to try this thing with the three of us, and I want to make it work. But you need to trust me."

I was caught between feeling intensely guilty for stalking him and intensely relieved that I'd learned exactly what I needed to know. So I nodded.

"Come into the restaurant, and I'll buy you a hummus and tomato on wheat and vegan potato salad with my employee discount. You can eat at the bar, and I'll hang out with you between customers." He pulled his hair up into a man bun.

I hopped out of the Jeep thinking things had turned out better than I expected.

CHAPTER 8
A NEW NORMAL

Free Verse Poetry by Danny D

"Close Encounters with the Toilet Bowl" a.k.a. "Swirlie"
Again my head's submerged.
"Of gayness you'll be purged,
You filthy, flaming, faggot, queer—
Are your cheeks wet with piss or tears?
Suck it up, like you suck dick
Or die—we don't give a shit."

Am I to drown?
Or be shamed till I back down?
Until I whimper and plead
And I beg them to be freed?
Appeals that fill their souls
With power and control.

Enough is never enough.
Into the bowl again, I'm stuffed.
They laugh as they lower me,
And I marvel at their cruelty.
I won't forget, nor will I forgive.
I marvel at my will to live.

Henry: My life

IT'S STARTING to be more normal with the three of us, but I don't think anyone looking from the outside would have a clue that anything has changed. We ride to school together like we always used to do, sit together at lunch, and hang out on the weekends as much as my parents will let us. No obvious changes.

But it's starting to *feel* different. It's softer between us. We listen more carefully and speak more sweetly to one another. And though we've never had another chance to be alone together long enough to get busy like we did on the night of the sleepover at Brody's house, we all really want to. But the deal got sealed that night, and now we don't worry as much about going back to just being friends.

The cafeteria is full, and Danny hasn't shown up. A month ago Brody and I would have figured that he met a middle-aged guy who swept him off his feet at the restaurant and Danny decided hanging with him was a better bet than coming to school. But that was then.

"What's up with Danny?" I ask. "Why isn't he here already?"

"I don't have a clue. He never said anything about being late. Maybe he's upstairs in the art lounge, talking to a teacher or something," Brody offers and lightly kicks my foot beneath the table. That's our way of holding hands, because we can't *actually* hold hands in public.

"Yeah, I guess." We pick at our food for the next ten minutes and wait for Danny, who never comes. Then I notice something disturbing. "Look. No-neck Nelson and Lionel Wagner aren't in their usual seats either."

"I have a bad feeling," Brody says, and he stands up. I grab his tray and mine, toss our trash, and follow him out of the cafeteria. "Where was his last class before lunch?"

"Upstairs in the art wing, I'm pretty sure." I passed by him right before fifth period, and that's where he was headed.

"Let's get up there, then."

We take the entire flight of stairs in three giant steps and head down the hall toward the teachers' lounge. The artsy kids and teachers eat lunch there together almost every day, except Danny, who eats with us. As usual Brody is the one to knock. I hang back.

Mr. Lansing, the youngish hipster art teacher, opens the door.

"Hi, Mr. Lansing. We're looking for Danny Denisco. Is he eating lunch up here with you?" Brody always does the talking with adults.

"Hmm…. He's not here, but I saw him just after fifth period. He was in the studio, checking on how his pottery project turned out after it was fired in the kiln. He stayed for a couple minutes and then said he was heading to lunch."

"Okay. Thanks a lot." Brody is always polite, but it's clear he's stressed.

"Was he not at lunch, Brody?" Mr. Lansing is crazy about Danny, and he looks worried.

"No, sir. He didn't show up, so we came here to look for him."

"I see. Well, he's in my sixth-period class, so I'll make sure he's accounted for then."

"That would be great," Brody says.

"In the meantime you two should probably get back to the cafeteria." Mr. Lansing gives us a stern teacher look that looks wrong on him because he's so cool, and he goes back into the lounge.

I follow Brody down the hall. "What do you think we should do now?"

"Find him." Brody says and breaks into a slow jog. I realize he's heading for the bathroom at the end of the hall. As I approach I hear the kind of sounds that go with a couple of assholes bullying an innocent victim.

"I think he's in the bathroom," I shout, but Brody's already on his way in. I bolt in behind him, and we see the broad, bent-over backs of two guys through the open door of the handicapped stall. "What the fuck are you doing?" I call out.

So much for a surprise attack.

Wagner and Nelson turn around but don't let go of the kid they're holding on to by the back of the neck, who I suspect is Danny.

"Let him go." Brody doesn't take the time to make a plan. He pushes his way right into the stall. Again I'm right behind him.

My heart sinks when I see exactly what I expect—Danny in the stall, crouched over the toilet, his hair and face soaking wet. Until that moment I thought swirlies in bathroom toilets were just stuff they put in movies to make the bullies look meaner. I was wrong. I toss Nelson out of the way and manage to slide in between Danny—who has crawled to the wall behind the toilet—and Wagner.

"Get outta my way, Perkins. I wasn't finished playing with my little dolly yet." He lunges forward, but I push him back as hard as I can.

"You wanna get to him? You're gonna have to go through me!" I yell, and it sounds fierce and furious and a little bit crazy.

No-neck Nelson seems to come to his senses. "Let's get out of here, Wagner. This isn't worth it."

But Lionel is furious that I made him stumble, and he's still itching to get his hands back on Danny. "You three are faggots—twisted, sick pervs—you know that?"

I yell right back, "Why do you give a shit?"

Brody grabs Lionel by the arm and tries to swing him in the direction of the door. But Lionel is twice as thick as Brody, and when he grabs Brody's arm and steps back, I know he's gonna take a swing.

I can't get there in time, so I shout, "Duck!"

Bad plan. When he hears my panicked voice, Brody turns to look at me and gets socked hard in the jaw, hits his head against the cement wall, and drops to the ground.

Danny, who's been silent to that point cries, "Jesus, Brody!" He scrambles out from behind the toilet and over to Brody's side.

Wagner and Nelson wisely decide it's time to bolt and leave me in the bathroom, five minutes before the start of sixth period, in the middle of a bad scene. Danny's hair and face drip with toilet water, and he rocks back and forth in an effort to calm himself. Brody is on the floor and conscious, but barely so.

"School's out for us today." They're too stunned to hear me, so I lean over and grab both of them by an arm. "We're leaving."

Brody and Danny struggle to get to their feet. I lead them out of the bathroom and down the hallway to the back stairs. We sneak down and out the rear of the building, and then we have to circle around to the other side of the school to get to the parking lot. When we get to the Jeep, I reach into Brody's front pocket and find his keys, unlock the Jeep, and help them in. Then I hop into the driver's seat and get us the hell off school property.

"You're gonna get caught cutting class, Henry...." Brody's voice is barely a whisper. "They'll call your parents."

I hand him my iPhone. "Send a text to the office that I have permission to leave school for a dentist appointment. And sign it Lenore Perkins." The school administration never questions me because I'm one of the "good" kids.

Brody seems to have trouble focusing on the phone, but a minute later, he says, "I did it."

"Danny, can you call your mother and ask her to excuse you for the afternoon?"

Danny's still rocking back and forth, but he has the presence of mind to answer. "I don't need to. I can text Mr. Lansing and tell him I felt sick and went home. He's cool. He'll excuse me from his class and cover me for my last class too."

"Good. Now, Brody. We have to send an email from your parents excusing you from classes."

Brody shakes his head and murmurs, "I'm done for the day. I have a study hall... and last period is... is a research session in the library. Ms. Joilet never takes attendance."

"So we're in the clear for the rest of our classes." I'm relieved that part of our challenge came together so easily. "Now we have to figure out where to go."

"My father's holding a senior-men's yoga class at our house this afternoon." Brody sounds apologetic, if foggy. "We can still go there, but we'll have to sneak past all the old dudes."

"My mother's down in Boston visiting some loser she met at the convenience store where she works. She's not coming home until the weekend," Danny says. "We can go to my place, but get me there quick. I'm friggin' disgusting, and I need a shower."

Danny keeps himself together, but I don't blame him for wanting to get under a stream of hot water. "Okay. We're on our way."

AN HOUR later we're sitting silently on Danny's twin bed, each consumed by our own thoughts. Danny brushes his long hair, which is wet from the shower, and Brody, who showered after Danny, seems to be dozing off.

"Decker, you might have a concussion. I think we should get you checked out at the hospital." I say it like I mean business, but he shoots me down.

"I've hit my head harder falling off my mountain bike… plenty of times."

"That doesn't make me feel any better, bro."

Danny hasn't said a word since he told us how dirty he felt in the Jeep. To get him to rejoin the land of the living, I ask, "How did you end up in that situation, you know, in the upstairs boys' room with Wagner and Nelson?"

"You mean with my head in the toilet?" He puts the brush on the little table beside his bed and curls up between Brody and me. It's a tight fit, but I like it.

"Yeah. What happened after fifth period?"

"Does it matter? The end goal of those assholes was to flush my head down the toilet, and they got what they wanted." He curls into a tighter ball.

Brody opens his eyes. "It matters," he says, but it seems like an effort for him to speak.

Something's different about Danny. He's sarcastic, as always, but still in shock. I think they got to him in a way that's not the same as our usual verbal sparring with the jocks in the cafeteria. They bullied him physically, and there's definitely a difference in his reaction. I put my hand on his shoulder, swallow my anger, and say what needs to be said. "You must have been really scared."

He unrolls from the tiny ball in order to sit up and stare at me. The look in his eyes isn't sweet and accepting. He's pissed off, and I hope not at me. "Ya think?"

"I mean, anybody would have been scared. I know I would have been," I add and hope that will make it better.

Danny's expression doesn't change. "You're six three and straight, as far as the rest of the school knows. You have no fucking clue how it feels to have your head submerged in toilet water and your hair sucked down as it's flushed, all while being called a filthy faggot."

He's right. I have no idea what he went through. Thankfully Brody finds the energy to slip into his typical fact-finder mode. "So, were they already in the bathroom when you went in, or did they drag you inside when you walked by?"

Brody receives a similarly hostile look from Danny. "I was already in there when they came in. They couldn't resist 'teaching me a lesson.' You see, I'm not a *real* boy, so I'm not supposed to use a boys' bathroom."

I swallow back my urge to jump off the bed and curse and stomp around the room. I murmur, "You're a real guy…." It's a stupid thing to say, even if it's true.

Brody is the one to get off the bed and try to make sense of what happened. "You've got to go to the principal about this." His words come out slowly, and he shakes his head as though to clear the cobwebs.

"Because Thomas Bailey Aldrich High School is a 'nonbullying zone'?" Danny laughs, and the sound is biting. "Yeah, right."

"We'll go with you. We're witnesses to what they did," Brody offers.

"No thanks." Danny drops back onto the bed and starts to roll into a ball again, but Brody reaches forward and stops him.

"Well, then, what do you want us to do?" he asks.

"You guys don't have to do anything, 'cause I'm not going back to school."

"What the fuck?" I ask as I see red and slip into the fury mode I've been resisting.

"I'm never going back there. You guys got that?" Danny closes his eyes and tries to dismiss us.

But Brody won't hear it. "We've got your back, Danny."

"You guys *can't* have my back. You've got no clue. I'm the only gay target at school."

"Then I'll come out," Brody blurts. "You won't be the only gay kid anymore." He looks at me.

I know he expects me to say I'll come out too, so the assholes at school will have to multiply their bullying efforts by three if they want to have an impact, but I can't tell him what he wants to hear. "I can't come out."

Danny sighs, but Brody doubles down. "Henry, we can make this easier on him."

"*Hello*! I'm *here*, and I'm *listening*." Danny gets pissed off when we talk about him like he isn't right next to us.

But I'm mad too. "Then sit up and talk to me. Hear what I have to say."

Danny obeys quickly. He sits up and pushes himself to the edge of the bed. "Go ahead. Say what you gotta say, King Henry."

I have Brody and Danny's full attention. Time to come clean. "I can't come out. If my parents learn I'm gay, they'll try to send me to one of those Christian conversion camps. Another family at my church sent their son, and Mom and Dad were all for it."

Brody shakes his head. "Those places don't work. Haven't you heard we were 'born this way'? Plus Perky, you're eighteen. You don't have to go anywhere you don't want to go."

I can't sit there any longer and hope they'll understand why it's impossible for me to come out. I hop off the bed and pace the room. "You just don't get it. This is my family… and I… it's like, I…."

Danny takes pity on me. "Sit down, Henry."

"But you don't get it."

"I get it." Danny's voice is firm but gentle. "I do. I've got no real family to lose by being gay or being Goth or… being whatever

I want to be." He stops and thinks for a second. "What I'm trying to say is that you have a lot to lose if you come out, and I don't want you to lose it for me."

Once again I feel like a knife is stuck in my gut. I'd do almost anything to look out for Danny, but I can't do that.

Brody changes his tune. "Then you don't need to come out, Henry. *I'll* come out and stand with Danny against those assholes."

"The jocks already think we're all gay," I say.

"No need to make it official so your folks find out," Brody insists.

I feel like a coward. *Maybe I am one.*

"So, Danny, will you come back to school? You need a diploma, especially if we all want to go to Prospect University together." Again Brody talks us down off the ledge.

"Shit." Danny flops back on the bed and drags the pillow onto his face.

"You can't hide from us, Danny," Brody persists.

"Okay. But... I'm... I'm kind of...."

Brody sits beside Danny, pulls the pillow away, and looks down on him. "I'm scared too, but we'll be doing this together."

Images of Brody and Danny holding hands in the hallways at school flash through my mind. *I can't be part of it. I can't be with them on this.*

"I guess I'll try," Danny says.

I'm relieved for Danny's sake, but the knife doesn't fall out of my side. It drives in another inch or two. "I've got both of your backs, and I mean it." My words sound lame, but I sit on Danny's other side and put my hand on his leg.

"Once we're at Prospect University together, this won't be an issue," Brody assures us, and then he pulls me and Danny backward, so we're lying crushed together on the little bed.

My parents will *never* accept that I'm gay, and if I come out, I'll run the risk of losing them. The immediate crisis seems to have been put to rest, though, so I try to relax. And when Brody, sensing my apprehension, reaches over Danny and touches the side of my face, I relax even more. He leans forward, and so do I, and we share a kiss that somehow begs me not to obsess over what can't be changed right now.

"Hey, let me into the party," Danny quips from beneath us, and we refocus on him. Brody goes for his lips, and I dive down to kiss his neck.

In the space of a few seconds, it's like I rocket from hell right up to heaven. We forget Danny's adventures in the art-wing bathroom and the way Brody's head bounced off the cement wall, as well as my crushing fear that Mom and Dad will find out who I really am.

"I want to feel your skin on mine," I admit in a surprisingly deep voice, and I rip my T-shirt over my head. Brody never put his shirt back on after his shower, so he's ready to go, and Danny's wearing a black bathrobe, which I open easily. We begin an exploration of one another's bodies that feels completely different from our first Saturday night together. Maybe it feels different because it's broad daylight and we can see every detail, or maybe it's because we're practically on top of one another in Danny's tiny bed. But I'd say it's different because we belong to one another now. That first night was awesome because it was a breakthrough, but now we confirm what we've got. We're moving forward in our relationship, with no doubts that this "thing" isn't real.

Free Verse Poetry by Danny D

> "Consuming Love"
> In their arms
> Tears dry,
> Hugs warm,
> Fears fly.
>
> Kisses heat,
> Arms hold.
> One boy sweet.
> The other bold.

Safety mine.
Pain banned
By a line
Drawn in sand.

One Reckless,
One Fuming,
One Defenseless,
Love Consuming.

Brody's notebook

THURSDAY, OCTOBER 23
    ~~My Big Fat Gay Diary~~
    Okay. So maybe this is *a fucking diary.*
    But here's what it isn't:
    My diary isn't flaming or rainbow-colored or speckled with glitter.
    And notable moments in life should be *documented in a diary. In my opinion it's the diary's primary function.*
    So here it is:
    I don't know that I am necessarily a gay man, but I just came out as one.

About the first part of the sentence above:
Growing up I never thought too much about what attracted me sexually or romantically to another person. Which is not to say I never had sexual or romantic feelings, because I have. But my attractions haven't been based on the same criteria as the other kids I knew, who obsessed over a girl because she had big boobs and was a total flirt, or a boy because he had nice biceps and was a good athlete. What I always experienced when I liked someone was an attraction to things I couldn't put my finger on. Maybe I liked the way someone looked

at me, or somebody's tone of voice. Or I admired a person's attitude about life or I related to someone's taste in music. Maybe we just laughed at the same types of jokes. But gender never factored into my feelings. I've liked both guys and girls.

And about the second part of the sentence—when it comes to my boyfriends, I might as well be strictly gay, because Danny and Henry are the only people I find hot and admire and laugh with. At least they are right now. And if supporting them means I come out of a closet that I've never really been stuck in, then that's what I'll do.

Danny ended up skipping school the day after he got dunked in the toilet. But he told us he was going to stay home ahead of time, so we were cool with it. He needed a day to get over his fear and find his inner strength. And the day after that, when he came back to school, I kissed him in the cafeteria.

Our plan was just to hold hands as we walked into the caf, because we thought it would send a strong enough message that we were together. And we carried out that plan—and everybody noticed. But when we sat down at our usual table beside the jocks, Danny looked so scared. He said he wasn't hungry and sort of shrunk into his seat. Henry was freaking out with guilt that he couldn't fix the situation, so I did what came naturally. I leaned over to Danny, who always sits beside me at lunch, and I planted a wet one on his lips.

And that was that.

I figured, why draw out speculation? Kissing Danny was kind of like saying to lunch block B, "We're here and we're queer, so you better get used to it."

There was a roar of chatter at the conclusion of our kiss. I don't think anybody missed it, least of all Lionel Wagner and his muscle-bound buddies. They yelled stuff at us.

"Whoa, baby." Jamie was the first to start in.

"Get a room!" No-neck shouted.

Lionel was loudest. "That's disgusting! Now I lost my appetite."

But once they simmered down, the jocks moved on to inhaling their lunches because it was meatloaf day, and apparently jocks appreciate a gravy-covered cake of ground beef. And they prefer to eat it warm.

The only one who seemed unable to get over the impact of our kiss was Henry. His eyes got an injured look. I wanted so much to lean across the table and kiss him too, but he'd said it couldn't happen because his parents might find out. I kicked his ankle underneath the table to let him know that he was an equal part of our relationship, but the hurt look didn't go away.

It's been a week now since I came out, and sure, it's been weird as hell, but Danny and I are already *almost* accepted as a couple at school. The teasing and bullying hasn't gotten worse. In fact I think maybe our openness is respected. The harassment has lessened. I also think Danny feels safer in the cafeteria and in the halls when he holds my hand.

I only wish Henry could hold on to us too.

Henry: My life

At first I didn't want to go. Who needs to go to some stupid Fall Festival where I'm going to look like a third wheel on Danny and Brody's bicycle, even if I'm not? But it's a benefit for the Spanish Club, and although Brody doesn't officially belong, he spends a lot of time at their meetings.

So Brody is going to the Fall Festival—after all, he organized it—and he wants Danny and me to meet him there. Even though Danny is his boyfriend in public, I'm his boyfriend too. So I'm gonna go and be supportive.

Tonight I get to use Mom's minivan because I'm going to a school-sponsored event. I pick up Danny and we head to the high school, where the courtyard has been decorated to celebrate autumn. There are haystacks to sit on, piles of leaves to jump in, and hot apple cider to drink. The place is mobbed with families from the town.

Brody's working at the pumpkin-carving station, and when he sees us, he comes over and breaks into a grin that makes me want to hug him, but only Danny can do that in public. Brody taps my toe with his hiking boot, and I know that's his way of hugging me. It mostly works. I feel hugged. He never lets me forget I'm part of them.

So I decide that tonight, in public, I'm gonna be Brody and Danny's boyfriend in every way, except in touching them. I promise myself I'll touch them later, when I get them alone.

Brody goes back to his place behind the long table and gives Danny and me a perfectly round pumpkin and a carving knife. Together we make a pumpkin that very loosely resembles Harry Potter. Danny could have made the pumpkin look real enough to cast a spell, but he insisted that I help.

"I don't think we stand a chance of winning. Look at the Sponge Bob pumpkin right there." I point three pumpkins down.

"Yeah. It's not bad, but neither is Harry," Danny argues.

As we're putting the scar on Pumpkin Harry Potter's forehead, Lionel and a group of his friends walk by. "Hey, Danny. Let us know if you have to take a piss. We'd be happy to escort you to the boys' restroom," Lionel bellows loudly enough for everybody at the pumpkin-carving table to hear, and I feel the heat in me rise as Danny wilts against my shoulder.

"Hope you're thirsty for toilet water," another guy yells.

Brody hears them too, which was probably the point. Ever since the bathroom incident and him coming out as Danny's boyfriend, Brody's been more protective of Danny. Brody drops his pumpkin and jumps over the table to get in Lionel's face.

"You better watch your step or I'll convince Danny to take a little trip to the principal's office. It's not too late to tell Mr. Marcotte about what you did to Danny in the bathroom that day. They won't let you play basketball, and you'll probably get expelled," Brody yells, even though Lionel is right in front of him.

"Dream on, Decker. No one's gonna say *boo* to Principal Marcotte if they want to see twenty."

"I'm not even nineteen yet, doofus," Brody replies.

I have to step in, because Brody's gonna get himself punched out again, and I'm not fully convinced he didn't get a concussion when his head hit the cement wall last time Lionel hit him. "Stay right here," I tell Danny, who flips me the bird for trying to boss him around. I walk over to where Brody's standing, surrounded by a wall of the school's biggest guys.

"Hey, Perkins. You here to defend your gay boy's honor?" No-neck asks.

"I'm here to tell the student volunteer at the pumpkin-carving table to get his ass back to his post. There's a bunch of little kids in a line waiting for pumpkins." I look pointedly at Brody.

"Oh, so it's time for *her* to get back to work? Is that what you're saying?"

"Shut up, Wagner, and move out of our way." I grab Brody by the arm and try to pull him back to where Danny's waiting. But when Lionel starts to mouth off again, Brody yanks his arm free.

"Let's go settle this out behind the school right now, Decker. Just you and me. We can kick each other's asses till one of us begs for mercy." Lionel isn't joking around, so I grab Brody's arm again and try to get him to come with me. Lionel outweighs Brody by at least thirty pounds and is four inches taller. It can't end well... for Brody, at least.

"Let's go, Wagner," Brody agrees, and in his eyes I see a frenzied look. It reminds me of his expression right before he ran down to the ocean at Branton Beach and got pummeled by waves.

So I grasp him by the shoulders, look into his eyes, and say, "Think about this, Brody. Think about Danny. He needs you in one piece. And I don't want you to get slapped around either. Come with me and leave this asshole in your dust."

Brody looks from me to Lionel. I know he craves the adrenaline rush he'd get from a fistfight. But he has to realize he'd get killed.

"Think it through," I add, hoping like hell he'll listen.

"But I want to pay him back for what he did to Danny." He tries to pull out of my grasp, but nonetheless continues to focus his gaze on my eyes. I think he hears me.

Next I tell Brody what he always tells me. "Take a deep breath, dude."

He actually does it and keeps staring at me.

"Are you coming or are you wimping out, Decker?" Lionel refuses to give up.

"He's not going anywhere with you." I don't look away from Brody. "Come on. Time to get back to your work station."

Brody nods and lets me lead him away. He's not a guy who worries about losing face for backing out of a fight. With Brody, adrenaline, not ego, is the issue at stake.

I turn around and say, "Stay the fuck away from Brody, Danny, and me. You got that?"

"Or what? What're you gonna do about it if I don't?" Wagner still won't let it go.

"I'll go to anybody and everybody who'll listen to me at this school to tell them what you and your friend did to mess with Danny in the upstairs bathroom."

"Oh no. Not that," No-neck squeaks in his high voice as we walk away, but I can tell he's worried.

When we get back to Danny and the pumpkin table, Brody snaps out of his trance. "I can't believe I didn't go fight him." He's stunned that he denied himself a chance to get a brutal but natural high.

"I'm glad," Danny says. "Take it from me. It sucks to kiss with a swollen lip."

For just a second, our hands come together between us, like we're playing that little kids' hand-stacking game. And it hits me hard. I'm not gonna be able to keep up the public farce that I'm just their pal forever. "I wish I could drive you home too," I say to Brody, knowing the plan is for me to take just Danny home.

"You can. I'll just leave my Jeep here and ask my dad to take me to get it in the morning," Brody replies. "So we can go out for ice cream before you drop us off."

"Sounds like a plan, so stay the fuck out of trouble until it's time to go," I warn.

"I'll try." He shrugs and grins. "You guys should go make a zombie scarecrow now. We're gonna decorate the front of the school with them. It's going to look like a zombie apocalypse at TBA High School."

"One more thing, Brody, don't even *look* at Lionel and crew if they pass you by, or you're gonna hear from me," Danny threatens. Then he turns and struts with purpose toward the big pile of leaves.

"Only if you think about reporting the asshole. Deal?" Brody calls after him, persistent too.

"I'll think about it," Danny shouts back, but I don't believe him. If you ask me, Danny doesn't think he deserves justice.

CHAPTER 9
AN ENTRY IN THE GRATITUDE JOURNAL

Brody's notebook

SATURDAY, NOVEMBER 29
My Gratitude Journal—just for today

Mom belongs to a group at the Cullfield Community House called the Gratitude Committee. They meet monthly, and from what Mom says, they make a lot of lists in their gratitude journals. Of course they list things they're thankful for, but they also list things they take for granted, modern technology they appreciate, life rituals that fulfill them, and they even list things they're not grateful enough for.

I think it's a good thing. And since it's Thanksgiving weekend, I'm going to take a page out of Mom's notebook.

Today I am grateful for:
1. Danny and Henry

I have to start with them. I might just end with them too. They're what I'd call all-important in my life. I don't know what I'd do without them.

2. This weekend

I thought the weekend was going to suck. Henry's parents signed his family up for a "Living Our Lives Fully in Christ" workshop, a thankfulness event at the Creator's Bible Church that started Thursday morning, went all day on Thanksgiving, and continued through the day Friday and into Friday night. It was "an adventure in marathon prayer," or so Henry said. They even slept as a group on cots in the church hall. Henry dreaded it, but he managed to survive.

In fact I'm really not sure how Henry feels about God and religion. I think if Mr. and Mrs. Perkins would stop stuffing God down Henry's throat, maybe he'd be able to decide what he believes and where that belief fits into his life. As it stands my best guess is that to Henry, going to church is a chore, loving God is an obligation, and learning his religion feels like brainwashing.

Danny had zero plans for Thanksgiving Day. His mother didn't even offer to drag him down to her new boyfriend's place in Boston. The restaurant was closed, so Danny celebrated his thankfulness alone.

My brother Tommy and his wife, Liza, were "doing" Thanksgiving this year in their condo at the ski resort they work at in Vermont. If there had been an early snow, it would have meant skiing—which is cool—even though there's no way the black-diamond trails could possibly be open in November. But the year has been dry and warm. Not even a single trail was open. I spent the day playing games on my phone and avoiding the turkey and the gravy made from turkey drippings that seemed to find its way into about everything on the table. There was salad—the staple of my existence. I hope they didn't drizzle it with turkey gravy too, because I ate it.

So, as a threesome, our prospects for sharing our gratitude were slim to none.

But maybe Henry prayed loudly enough for God to hear, because he got the okay from his parents to spend Saturday with Danny and me. Danny had to call in sick to work, but he didn't even hesitate. So after a Thanksgiving Day apart, we got to spend Saturday together.

3. The cliff on Butternut Mountain

This probably sounds like a strange thing to be thankful for, but the three of us spent the entire day Saturday on Butternut Mountain. The weather was so perfect, not at all like late fall, almost winter. It was sunny and cool, with enough of a breeze to make *me* feel alive, but not so much to make Danny and Henry think they would blow off the mountain. We picked up sandwiches at the local sub shop instead of Subway—it was Small Business Saturday—and then we drove to the base of the mountain, where a bunch of other cars were parked. We weren't the only ones who wanted to go for a hike rather than to a mall on the Saturday after Turkey Day.

We climbed the mountain on a trail that wasn't too steep and passed plenty of families. I thought I saw a few members of the Seniors Climb group that my parents sometimes hike with. The top of the mountain is cool, because it's actually a little bit scary. It's mostly sloped granite, but there are a few places that jut out beyond the rest of the rock. There's potential for a serious fall if you don't watch your step.

The three of us climbed onto a section of rock that jutted out about three feet, which made us feel like we were suspended midair. We ate our subs, sucked down bottles of water, and didn't say too much.

Danny's a little bit scared of heights, and since the mountain is three towns away from Cullfield, Henry wasn't scared to reach out and put his hand on Danny's knee. I loved seeing that. I put my hand on Henry's back, which linked us all together.

After we ate, all three of us stretched out on the rock, put our hands on one another's arms, and stared at the bright blue sky. It was so peaceful, I never wanted to leave.

"If there were ever a blizzard," I remember saying without even thinking, "I'd want to come right here. Picture what the snow would look like, swirling around in the air and then falling in our faces."

"I think I can live without *that* experience," Danny said, and he squeezed my hand hard, like he did that windy day on Branton Beach.

Then Henry had a good idea. "When there's a blizzard, we should go sledding on Welker Hill."

You can pick up a decent amount of speed on Welker Hill if you wax the runners of your sled, so I guess it would be cool. But that spot on the mountain, with the wind gusting and snow spraying and my feet freezing… well, even if it were great, it probably wouldn't be safe.

Maybe it would be a better option to go sledding with Danny and Henry. I could bring a thermos of hot chocolate.

4. Family

Mom for the gratitude-journal idea, Dad for regular Dad things—paying bills, giving me the Jeep with no questions asked, taking care of business—and my six brothers, their six wives, their eleven children, and the ones on the way, because they exist too.

5. If I had a dog, I'd be thankful for him. I'd name him Brody to confuse everybody. Just picture me walking around my neighborhood, yelling, "Here, Brody. Come here, Brody." LOL. But when we're alone, I'd call him my Little Bro.

6. Danny and Henry

Brody's notebook

WEDNESDAY, DECEMBER 10
~~Diary of an Accepted Prospect University Student~~
OMG! OMG! OMG! We all got in!!!!! AAAAHHHHH!!!!!!

Today was the best day of my life so far. At lunch, when I checked my email, there was a message from Prospect University. I told Danny and Henry, and they took out their phones. They had emails too.

We opened them at the same time, which would have sucked if one of us didn't get in, but we all read the word *Congratulations* at the same time. And we all screamed. Well, we didn't actually scream out loud. It was a silent scream, as Henry values his reputation, and Danny values his life. I don't value either of those things, but I went along with keeping my joy silent.

But we're in. We can be together next year… and for the next four years.

I ought to go back to the gratitude-journal page and add a thank-you for that.

Christmas came early for me this year.

Free Verse Poetry by Danny D

Accepted.
Wanted by strangers
Who think they know
Enough to judge,
Because I showed them
The pictures inside me.

Accepted.
Feeling honored
That I'm called gifted.
But who was there
When I was wretched?
The two who share me.

Henry: My life

OH GOD, we all got into Prospect University. Sometimes you get what you wish for… what you pray for.

Now what the fuck am I gonna do?

Mom and Dad are gonna go ballistic. If I tell them about it right now, they'll have me down at the church within five minutes, begging God for forgiveness for my disobedience.

But I want this. I want it as much as I want Danny and Henry.

And as a NCAA Division Two College, I can get an athletic scholarship. The Prospect U track coach emailed me to let me know that it will be "substantial," and the information will be emailed to me soon.

Danny also got a merit scholarship for his excellence in art, and while it isn't "substantial," it will help.

And Brody. There aren't words for how happy he is. I think it would be harder to tell him I'm *not* going to go to Prospect, than it would be to tell my parents I *am* going to Prospect.

Prospect U has an awesome new athletic coaching program that I'm really into.

I want this. And isn't it my life? What the fuck am I gonna do? What the fuck am I gonna do?

Brody's notebook

WEDNESDAY, DECEMBER 17
    ~~*Becoming Us*~~
    "Becoming Us" has a nice ring to it.
    I have a lot on my mind, and I hope I can dump it all here so I'll be able to study for my Physics test. And so I can breathe again. And eat something. And sleep tonight.

I'm worried because Henry hasn't told his parents that he got into Prospect University. I'm sure he's as excited as we are, but he has to hide it from his parents because Prospect isn't D1 in Men's Track or a Christian school—which is so freaking ridiculous. Henry's an adult. He can make his own choices, but his parents won't let him.

Danny's shocked that he got into Prospect, but it's slowly sinking in. For the first time, he's starting to get that he's worth something—and not just to Henry and me, but to a great college that's offering him money to study art.

During the week between Christmas and New Year's Eve, there's an overnight for accepted-Early-Action students. Henry's going to have to tell his parents if he wants to go. He knows that as well as we do, but he refuses to talk about it. Henry acts as though it will go away if he ignores the need to tell them.

On a positive note, since Danny's eighteenth birthday is Friday, Henry and I are going to take him to the Galleria of Ink to get his "I'm

With Them" tattoo on his left wrist. I know Henry wants one too. Maybe when we get to Prospect University, he'll feel free enough to get it. He'd look so hot with "I'm With Them" on his bicep. And it would be more proof that this thing with us is real.

We're going to have our own private Christmas party this weekend since there's no chance we'll be able to see one another on actual Christmas Day. Brothers, wives, nieces, and nephews will be coming to my house, and Henry will be ingesting a high dosage of Christian holiday music and prayer. Danny will probably spend Christmas alone, like he did Thanksgiving. I don't want to think about that.

Got to sign off and study.

CHAPTER 10
SEASON'S GREETINGS

Free Verse Poetry by Danny D

"Handmade"
String lights sparkle,
Tree stars glitter.
All that shines was made from litter.
Caps and corks from kitchen trash,
Last year's candy—prices slashed.
Our tree I dug, our nest secondhand,
But nothing that they see is bland.
Gray eyes see hope,
The dark fear God.
My light ones only see the flaws.
But in the gentle Christmas glow,
All things wicked we forego.
We face ourselves.
We face each other:
A family without a father or mother,
Thrown away, cast off in the storm.
Still there's beauty in things well-worn,
And what is dull, that which is frayed,
I'll paint, I'll sew,
Rebirth handmade.

Brody's notebook

SATURDAY, DECEMBER 20
~~The Christmas Story~~
I can't let this go by without writing about it.

I just got back home after celebrating with Danny and Henry. For the record it was a private Christmas party at Danny's house. But in reality it was more a celebration of what the three of us have together. I'm not too religious, but there was something almost spiritual about tonight. I think all of us felt it.

Christina Denisco has been gone as much as my parents lately. I don't think Danny misses her company at this point, but he has worries that I don't have. "Did Mom pay the rent? And what about the electric bill?" and, "Am I supposed to buy all of my own food when I'm trying to save for college?"

On the bright side, we had his apartment to ourselves.

Danny organized the whole evening, and all he asked was that Henry and I bring something to eat for dinner and that we bring ourselves—but no gifts.

When we got to his place, we stuck the Chinese food in the refrigerator, and he invited us to his room. In the middle of the bedroom, on an upside-down, blue plastic bin, sat a little fir tree in a red burlap sack. Danny handed Henry a string of lights and said, "Go to town, Perkins."

As Henry wrapped the lights around the tree, Danny handed me a puffy, bright green comforter that looked out of place among all the black decorations in his room.

"Spread it out on the floor," he told me, and then he turned away to mess with his phone. Soon a very strange version of "All I Want for Christmas is You" filled the room.

Henry and I looked at each other and shrugged.

"My Chemical Romance," Danny told us, which explained the music.

I nodded and asked, "So it's going to be a punk-rock Christmas Party?"

Danny winked at me. "Wait till you hear the rest of the playlist."

Once I spread out the blanket, Danny brought over a fancy shoebox covered in Christmas wrapping paper. He knelt down and opened it.

"What's all this?" I asked him.

"Ornaments." Danny then rolled his eyes and said, "Duh," like only he can.

Henry and I knelt down on either side of him and watched as he took all the tiny ornaments out of the box and placed them in rows on the bedspread.

"What the fuck? You said no gifts." Henry seemed kind of pissed off.

But Danny came back with a decent excuse. "They're not *real* gifts. I made them."

"They're still gifts," Henry mumbled, but his eyes got teary. He quickly blinked the tears away.

There were yarn wreaths tied with red and green ribbons and little snowmen made of bottle caps that he'd painted white. Danny made tiny light bulbs look like penguins and even decorated wine corks to resemble reindeer. Danny told Henry that he hardly had to buy anything because there were so many wine corks and bottle caps in his kitchen trash.

Henry and I looked over the ornaments for a few minutes. We could tell Danny put a ton of work into making them.

Then Danny told us, "After you put them on the tree, I've got something else for you."

Henry and I were obedient. We moved to the tree and hung the ornaments while Danny grabbed a plastic bag off his bed and dumped out ten small candy canes.

"We can each eat one, but the others get hung on the tree. K?"

"Sounds fair," Henry said as he unwrapped a candy cane and started to suck on it. I did the same, and then we hooked the others over the branches. As soon as we'd done that, Danny passed us each a handful of tinsel and nodded toward the tree like he meant business, so we went to work.

After the tree was decorated, Danny got up and went to his top dresser drawer. He pulled out a delicate yellow star made of folded paper. When he held it out so we could see, he said, "I wrote all of our names on it with a gold calligraphy pen."

He'd written our first and last names all over the yellow star so they overlapped and intersected. "That's amazing." My words didn't do his art or his effort justice.

I think we all knew that if Henry tried to say anything, he'd make one of those choking noises. So it was okay that he stayed quiet.

We studied the star for a few more seconds, and then Danny placed it at the top of the tree, stepped back, and sighed loud enough for us to hear over the Anti-Queens singing "I Saw Daddy Kissing Santa Claus."

"Now lie down." Danny was clearly in charge of the night. He tossed us a couple of pillows from his bed and turned out the lights in the room, and we stretched on the bright green comforter to gaze at the sparkling tree. Very somberly he said, "Merry Christmas," and I knew that it already was.

Henry: My life

MY FAMILY isn't doing the present-swapping thing this year for Christmas, which is fine with me. I have everything I need. Instead of buying one another gifts, Mom, Dad, and I are donating the money we would have spent to StJude.org to help end childhood cancer. It's a great cause, but I must be selfish, because Christmas feels different without secretly shopping for gifts and wrapping them up. And even though the idea of Santa Claus is ancient history, I miss the magical feeling of wondering what will be waiting for me under the tree on Christmas morning.

Except for the awesome night Brody, Danny, and I spent decorating a little tree in Danny's bedroom, Christmas is a total downer this year. It's come down to tonight—Christmas Eve—for me to fill in Mom and Dad on my awesome/horrifying news about my acceptance to a non-D1, non-Christian college.

"Wasn't the Christmas Eve service wonderful, Carter? Reverend Wilson certainly knows how to inspire us to find it in our hearts to give." Mom is totally captivated by the new reverend at the Creator's Bible Church. And he *is* inspiring. I've got to give him that. But I'm inspired to do things with my life other than what involves strictly centering my life on Jesus Christ.

I think I'd like to be a coach someday, but not necessarily at a Christian boys' school like Mom and Dad would want. And I'd like to have two male partners share my life with me, which is certainly not prescribed by the good Reverend Wilson.

"Yes, Lenore. Reverend Wilson speaks to my soul, as well. And Henry, I think he'll be a perfect person to write one of your college recommendations."

The three of us sit around our shiny dining room table, eat a formal holiday roast beef dinner and all the fixings off our best china, and as usual, discuss how religion factors into my life. It's not a great way to introduce my upcoming, and very secular, retreat to Prospect University.

"What a wonderful idea. Henry, Reverend Wilson has been witness to many of your volunteer activities at the church. He knows your capacity for kindness because he sees you interact with the children at Sunday school lessons as well as with the elderly when you play sports games with them."

"Yeah… um… about that…. About college…." *So far, so bad.*

"Have you given any more thought to attending a divinity school?" Mom asks, her eyes sparkling. She'd like me to attend a Christian college to pursue *her* goals for me. Dad has other ideas.

"I thought we discussed this, Lenore. Our top priority is that Henry reach his potential as an athlete at a Division One college track program. This path will most glorify God by making use of his gift. Remember how several college coaches came to Henry's track meets last spring to see him run?" Dad is on a roll, and he's rolling right over Mom and me. "Henry's track coach, Bob Wilmot, reached out to two more schools on his behalf last summer. And I've been in contact with about five other university coaches as well. The interest is there. We just need to keep the lines of communication open."

Mom and Dad eye each other over the mashed potatoes. "Henry tells me he's already working on applications to several excellent Bible colleges," Mom points out.

"*And* to NCAA Division One schools as well, dear."

It's now or never. "And I've been accepted early action to attend Prospect University," I blurt and quickly stuff a forkful of overcooked carrots into my pie hole.

My parents' mouths drop open in unison. They couldn't have performed better if they'd practiced. And then, in one voice, they ask, "What are you talking about?"

I keep chewing the carrots. No talking with my mouth full is a rule, and I intend to follow it.

"Henry, what is this foolishness?" Dad actually pushes back from the table and gets to his feet.

Mom lifts her napkin from her lap and dabs at her forehead and upper lip.

I swallow the carrots and then do my best to swallow back my fear. "I sent in an early action application to Prospect University. They offer a great coaching program… and I'm… interested… in it."

Mom sways in her chair as if she's about to faint. I should rush to her side, but I'm frozen to my seat.

"Prospect University is out of the question, Henry," Dad states and points at me. "It was not on my list or your mother's list of colleges."

"It was on *my* list." My voice is soft and squeaky, like Danny's when he's guilty.

Dad throws his napkin onto the table.

I decide to bite the bullet and finish it. *Why draw out the pain?* "And the Prospect University Accepted Early Action Student Overnight is this week from Monday night until Wednesday afternoon."

Mom shakes her head. "It's a shame you *will not* be attending, son."

I shake *my* head. "I… but I really want to check it out."

"I would wager that one of those *boys* at school who you call *friends* has convinced you to engage in this folly," Dad argues.

"It has nothing to do with them," I lie. "And I have RSVP'd to Prospect U that I'll be going."

Christmas Eve dinner is over. Dad storms off into the living room and Mom sniffs back tears.

"Very well, son," she says, refusing to look at me. "But maybe you need to spend some time between now and then considering God's commandment to honor one's parents." She stands, picks up her plate, and heads toward the sink.

I feel like the Grinch who stole Christmas, but I said what I had to say, and I'm going to visit Prospect U this week with Brody and Danny.

But I have a feeling I'm in for a very chilly Christmas Day.

CHAPTER 11
THREE-THING

Free Verse Poetry by Danny D

"Three-thing"
In this three-thing,
Who is the hill's king?
Both take away life's harsh sting.
One same melody us three sing,
Shielded under caring wing,
Eternal hope in me does spring.
Far beyond a hollow fling,
A sturdy vine to which we cling.

Brody's notebook

TUESDAY, DECEMBER 30
~~The Gay Days of Our Lives~~
Henry, Danny, and I are at the Prospect University Accepted Student Overnight. I'm taking a second by myself to write this down while Henry and Danny grab us a couple pizzas. I just don't want to forget.

I was surprised when I woke up this morning and I wasn't in my bed. I was even more surprised when I opened my eyes and saw a very close-up view of tight, black curls. Henry's scalp was

126

so close to my nose I could smell his Henry smell. He was still out cold, though, with his sweaty forehead plastered to my left shoulder. The frosting on the cake was my right hand curved around Danny's chest—as in, I was holding on to his right pec. Like it was a boob. On top of his T-shirt, but still, it was a surprising situation to find myself in.

I made the unsurprising choice to stay as still as a tree—you know, on a day with no wind—because I want to make the closeness last.

But soon I had to fight the urge to stretch. I tend to be overly active, and stretching out my muscles when I wake up is a habit that has apparently turned into a need. Plus you can't fart when you're in close quarters like that, and the amount of beans I consume as a protein source leads to excessive gas. On top of all that, nature called my name because I sucked down every last drop of an extra-large caramel soy latte right before we fell asleep on the common-room floor. But since I was caught between a rock and a hard place, or, more accurately, between the forehead and right pec of my two boyfriends, I didn't move a muscle. And I tried like hell to enjoy that moment of unexpected intimacy—even if I was the only one awake to enjoy it.

At that point Henry rubbed his nose against my bicep. It was memorable enough to write down because of how completely un-Henry-like it was—so spontaneous and unaware. And again I was surprised.

Then my hand—the one cupped over Danny's pec—involuntarily flinched. It wasn't a boob squeeze. I was *not* feeling him up. It was merely an unintentional and unified movement of all my finger muscles, probably a result of my fierce need to pee. I knew that if I didn't answer nature's call, I was going to embarrass myself in a very wet way, which wasn't how I wanted to start an accepted-student overnight at my first—only—choice college.

So I tried to slide my hand off Danny's chest as my first move to extricate myself from that awesome tangle.

"Stop fidgeting," Danny murmured.

"I've got to pee. I've *almost* waited too long." I decided to be brutally honest.

"Jesus," he said and rolled away from me.

I took advantage of the moment, slid out, and headed to the bathroom.

The three of us were staying in a three-bedroom, one-bathroom suite in a huge brick dormitory at Prospect University. Although we requested to be placed in the same suite, we'd each been assigned to share a room with a stranger, so we ended up sleeping on top of Henry and Danny's sleeping bags with my sleeping bag draped over us on the common-room floor, instead of in our assigned bunk beds. The floor was hard and uncomfortable, but the company made up for it. We didn't think there was enough privacy to fool around, but being close to one another all night long was good enough—not that we weren't all horny as hell by the time we fell asleep.

When I got back to the common room, Henry was awake.

"Morning, Perky. Hmm... you don't look too perky," I said to him.

"I'm hungry, I guess," he said, but I knew that coming with us was hard for Henry to do. But he did. For the first time, Henry told his parents what he was going to do, instead of the other way around, and they didn't like it one bit. I'm pretty sure he's still dealing with having bucked their authority, because Henry's a pleaser, and all he ever wanted was to make his parents proud—until we became *us*. And now there's something he wants more.

"You sure you're doing okay?" I dropped onto the nest of sleeping bags, right beside where Henry was lying on his belly, and put my hands on the bare skin of his back. It felt so weird that I could do that, but Henry's mine, and I can touch him if I want. As long as no one wanders into the common room and catches us.

I rubbed his back, and he moaned softly, which was the lure that drew Danny in. Danny slid over so he was on his belly right beside Henry, and he put an arm across Henry's lower back. I moved one hand to Danny's shoulder and squeezed. It was amazing to have Henry's big muscles under one palm and Danny's wiry ones under the other—and to know they were both mine.

While grinning like an idiot, I rubbed their shoulders for a couple minutes, and listened carefully for the sounds of the other guys, but it stayed quiet. Henry pulled me down, and I ended up in the middle with both of them leaning over me.

"It's worth it. This is worth anything." Henry looked at Danny and then at me after he said that, and his expression was so sincere I believed he meant it. Then he put his lips on mine and kissed me like he was a sailor who'd just returned from a year at sea.

Danny pulled my sleeping bag back over our heads as though that would assure us privacy. If the other guys came out of their rooms, they'd know exactly what we were up to, but I didn't care. He slid his hand right down into the front of my sweats, grabbed my dick, and went to work on me. Kissing Henry, getting jerked off by Danny…. It was so good. I just lay back and let it happen.

Henry's kisses moved off my lips and down my neck, and when he started to suck on my right nipple, I let go in Danny's hand.

I immediately knew I needed to make them feel the same way, so I turned to kiss Danny, and his lips were just right—soft and wet. I reached out and took their dicks in my hands and returned the most awesome favor.

It was epic, if not a little bit rushed because we didn't want to get caught.

By the time the other guys got up, we were showered, dressed, and casually sitting around the common room on the stiff chairs, waiting for breakfast. The common room didn't even smell like sex anymore.

Henry: My life

IT'S FUCKED-UP to be feeling so happy and so miserable at the same time. But since I'm away from home and the two people who make me miserable, I focus on being happy and go with it. What happened with Danny and Brody this morning made coming here worth Mom and Dad's pissed-off looks and the silence and the guilt.

What isn't awesome about waking up next to your two favorite people and then kissing them and touching them and getting off with them? Danny and Brody make me forget about the expectations I'm supposed to live up to and let me just live.

I really like Prospect University too, even though the three of us spent the day apart. We explored the school, checked out the different majors, and even talked to the mentoring students who already go here.

I learned that the coaching program is just a minor, but I could do it with a major in either sports management or athletic training. I spent the day at the Hodges Sports Complex, and it was everything I wanted it to be. Now I'm at the dining hall, waiting for Brody and Danny to come back from their college-major explorations—Danny at the Art Department, and Brody at the Adventure Education Program.

"Henry!" My name erupts out of Danny's mouth when he sees me, and it makes me feel like I'm the man. "Henry, I love the Art Department here. It has all the stuff I want. They offer ceramics and drawing and graphic design… and they even offer an art-teacher education program. I don't know how I'm gonna decide."

Danny never acted like he deserved an education. Even when he was accepted to Prospect, he treated it like some kind of fluke. But tonight, he believes it. And he can see his future here. "You don't have to decide yet, do you?"

"No… I don't even have to let them know until the end of freshman year. And I talked to the lady at financial aid. She said that, with my scholarship and some student loans, I can afford this. I can go here." The eager smile looks odd on Danny's face. He usually appears totally bored.

"This is great. You *so* deserve it, Danny." I can't help but look around for Brody.

"I saw Brody a minute ago. He stopped to talk to the Environmental Science Department representative."

"Cool. Let's wait for him before we get our dinner."

IT COULD HAPPEN

It's nice to sit at a table in a public cafeteria and not have to prepare myself for insults from the next table over. Once again I get a picture of the kind of freedom Prospect University offers us. And when Brody charges into the dining hall, looking about as excited as Danny did, I'm sure it's the right place for us.

At dinner we're freer with one another than we've ever been at TBA High School. It's as though we somehow know that our future is here, and we're not going to be forced to spend the next four years hiding our feelings for one another from the rest of the student body. So when Brody reaches across the table and touches my hand and lets the touch linger, I don't pull my hand away. And nobody at the surrounding tables seems to care what we're doing, because they're all so involved with what *they're* doing. When Danny and Brody lean into each other and their foreheads come together, they look natural and comfortable.

I want the education we can all get here, but it's more than that. I want the freedom to be with Brody and Danny that this school will give us.

I guess I want the freedom to be me.

"Let's do this," I say out of nowhere.

Danny and Brody look across the table at me. Their smiles fall, and they look confused. Danny's the one to ask, "Do what?"

"I want the three of us to come here next year," I say, hardly believing my own words.

"You need to think this through, Perky, and convince your parents." Brody's trying to be the voice of reason, but he can't hide his excitement. His eyes are as round as silver dollars.

"I know what I want," I reply. "And one more thing."

They look across the table at me and wait for the rest of what I have to say.

"It's time for us to go public at Thomas Bailey Aldrich High School."

My boyfriends look at each other and then back at me.

"Say *what?*" Brody asks.

"I'm talking about us going public as a threesome."

"Henry, are you feeling okay?" Danny uses sarcasm to cover his surprise. He even reaches across the table and puts his hand on my forehead. "You haven't got a fever."

"I'm fine. I'm absolutely fine. I'm just sick of hiding."

"And I'm sick of taking crap from assholes," Danny says. "If we come out as a threesome at school, I'm not gonna let anybody mess with me and get away with it. I've had enough of being everybody's whipping boy."

"If one of those assholes tries to take you down—" I start.

"I'm gonna book it to Principal Marcotte's office," Danny finishes my thought and folds his arms over his chest.

I feel better about coming out, knowing Danny's done taking crap and keeping quiet about it.

Brody smiles too, and he reaches across the table. I grasp his hand and then go so far as to bring it up to my lips. A few kids from nearby tables look over at us—their eyes flickering over my lips on Brody's skin—but they don't seem to give a shit.

"I want to attend school here if you guys do," he says.

"We can request a triple. There are about ten triples in the freshman dorms." Danny still wears the expression of a kid at Disneyland. "I asked, and the housing representative said they'd show them to us tomorrow."

It feels like a dream is unfolding in front of me. And I'm sure I can be the guy they deserve—the guy I really want to be. "Sounds like a plan. Now let's go see if the food here is as good as everything else," I suggest and stand up.

Brody's notebook

WEDNESDAY, DECEMBER 31—*a depressing New Year's Eve*
  ~~Shit That's Hard to Talk About but Easy to Write~~
  ~~I am Brody, Hear Me Roar~~
  What happened next:

IT COULD HAPPEN

We just got back from Prospect University. I dropped Henry and Danny off at their houses, and I already feel empty—like we just left our heavenly future to come back to the crappy present.

It's New Year's Eve, so we have about eight months left until we can go back to heaven and stay there. Hopefully the time will pass quickly. I can keep myself busy with all the clubs I don't belong to. And Danny plans to work as many hours as he can so he can take the least possible amount of money in loans to get through college.

Henry's the weak link. His parents are going to freak out when he tells them he wants to go to Prospect University, as it isn't Division One or Christian. On Tuesday night, when we went for a long walk around campus, he told us he could handle it.

He said, "I've gotta grow up and tell them what I want out of life, at some point. If I don't do it now, I'm gonna end up going to a school they pick for me. And that means without you guys."

Danny looked as worried as I felt. He pointed out, "They've put a lot of time and effort into all of your sports and into bringing you up in your church, Henry. I don't think they're gonna take it very well."

"They're gonna have to." Henry said it like he meant it, but I don't know.

AND THE other major thing on my mind… I'm pretty sure I love Danny and Henry.

I haven't told them because I don't want to scare them off. And who knows? Maybe I'm wrong about being in love. I wasn't sure I could be in a relationship with guys until I dove into actually being gay with Danny and Henry. Maybe the way I think I feel about them is something else and not love at all.

CHAPTER 12
TOO GOOD TO BE

Henry: My life

I'M OUT.

Oh God, I'm out.

I came out at school.

It wasn't anything I said. It's 100 percent what I'm doing right now. Sitting at lunch with Danny and Brody, I just reached across the table and took one of each of their hands in mine. I plan on staying like this until it's our turn to grab some food.

Not that I'll be able to eat a bite, because *nobody* has missed my big move into multiple-partner gay love.

Shit.

Or not.

Everything's different now.

I'M STANDING in the hallway outside the locker room, and I'm having one hell of a hard time forcing my ass in there so I can change my clothes for basketball practice. News at TBA High School travels damned fast. By now everybody knows I'm gay. And everybody knows I'm in a gay threesome. The guys are gonna be all over me.

I don't know if I can deal with it.

I swallow hard, lift up my head, and remind myself that I'm the starting center on the team and they need me more than I need them. Then I step forward into what I've chosen.

IT COULD HAPPEN

PRETENDING TO read *The Great Gatsby*, I'm sitting alone in the front seat of the late bus to head home after basketball practice. Which I survived. Nobody said anything about me being part of a gay threesome—at least not in actual words. They were probably too fucking stunned to verbalize their thoughts. But nobody would have a thing to do with me.

They wouldn't change their clothes near me.

They wouldn't pass to me.

They wouldn't look at me.

They certainly wouldn't shower near me.

I'm not sure what I've done to my life.

WHEN I come into the kitchen, everything's quiet—too quiet. Usually dinner is cooking in a Crock-Pot or simmering on the stove, especially on Tuesdays, because it's Bible Study night. And since both of my parents' cars are in the driveway, it makes no sense that they aren't in the kitchen, getting ready for dinner.

I drop my backpack by the door and toe off my sneakers, because shoes aren't allowed in the house, according to the "cleanliness is next to godliness" rule. "Mom? Dad?" I shout.

They don't answer, which is weird. Maybe they're still mad because I went to the overnight at Prospect University last week. They haven't said much to me since I got home, but I figured they needed time to get used to the fact that I'm starting to make decisions for myself.

"Are you guys home?"

"In the living room," my father calls. "Please come in here."

I walk down the hall, and as soon as I see them, I know that something is drastically wrong. Mom has a box of tissues on her lap and is crying into one. Dad is sitting next to her on the couch, hands on his knees, and staring straight ahead.

"What's wrong?" *Who died?*

Mom sobs. My heart starts to pound.

"I think you know what's wrong, Henry," Dad replies. His voice is cold.

My mouth gets dry. "Dad...."

"Be quiet." He stands up, crosses the room to look out the window, and carefully avoids catching my eye. "We want you to leave."

"*What*? What are you talking about?"

"Just get out, Henry!" Mom screams and falls to her side on the couch.

I'm glued to my spot in the doorway of the living room. Part of me knows I should go to her, hug and comfort her, but I don't. "Mom... what did I do?" I can't slow down my thoughts enough to make sense of the situation.

Dad storms over to me and gets right in my face. I had no idea he could move so fast. He looks into my eyes and then grabs me by the shoulders and shakes me hard. "You are living your life in sin, you are an abomination, and you are no longer welcome in this home." He pushes me into the doorframe, and my head knocks hard against the wood. An image of Brody's head as it smashed against the cement wall in the boys' bathroom flashes in my mind. I'm dazed, but I hear the rest of what he has to say. "People with morals don't *do* the disgusting things you are doing with those two boys."

I'm afraid to guess exactly what I did to upset them, because I fear I may give up my secret. But I'm fairly sure they already know about Brody and Danny and me. "Who told you?"

"Your basketball coach saw you and your *friends* at lunch today. He said you three were all holding hands. Thank God the man had the good grace to call me at work and inform me."

"That... what he saw... it wasn't real. We were just pulling a fast one on Lionel Wagner." I lie so easily. It just slips right out. "It was just a joke."

"Don't compound your sinfulness by lying to us." Mom finds the presence of mind to speak. "You may have five minutes to take what you need from your room, and then we want you out of this house." She refuses to look at me.

Dad crosses the room and sits next to Mom.

"Mom… Dad… this can't be happening…."

Mom screams at me, her voice shrill. "What you are doing—a repulsive sin with *two* men—is the thing that *can't* happen! Now, go!"

"You heard your mother. You have five minutes."

Brody's notebook

TUESDAY, JANUARY 6

I've never seen Henry the way he was last night when he showed up on my front step.

Luckily I was the one to answer the door when he knocked, because Mom would have taken one look at him and called an ambulance. He was holding on to his chest with one hand like he was having a heart attack, and he had a heavy backpack over his other shoulder. He could barely stand. I asked, "Henry, what's up? Are you sick?"

He lifted his head and looked at me. His eyes were puffy and red and wet.

"How did you even get here?" I asked.

Henry opened his mouth to say something, but nothing came out. So I decided it was time to take him up to my suite. My parents would ask questions if they saw him in that condition. Henry had trouble on the stairs, but I managed to get him up there.

"Lie down on the bed, Perky. I'm gonna call Danny." I figured it was as much Danny's place to know what was going on as it was mine. Plus I needed his support.

Henry dropped down on my bed and rolled onto his side, but didn't say a word.

I called Danny and told him to get right over to my house. Then I sat on the bed next to Henry and rubbed his shoulders and neck until Danny arrived.

I'm normally the fact finder in our threesome. It's my specialty. But I felt shaky, having dealt alone with Henry for the past half hour. Luckily Danny stepped up to the plate and asked some pertinent questions. "Look, Henry, we can't help you unless you tell us what's going down. So what happened?"

Henry rolled onto his back and looked up at us with his swollen, dripping eyes.

"Is it your parents? Did something happen with them?" Danny asked.

Henry nodded, but when his forehead wrinkled up, we both looked away. Neither of us wanted to see him sob.

"Do they know about us?" Danny asked the obvious.

When Henry nodded I cut in. "So… what did they do to you?"

"Kicked me out…." Henry's voice was little more than a ragged whisper.

"Jesus," Danny muttered.

"The reason they kicked you out was because you're gay?" I wanted to figure out the details.

"Sinful…," Henry whispered.

And then Danny was on top of him. "You're not sinful, Henry. *They're* sinful for calling you that."

When Henry shook his head, I jumped on the bed too, and Danny and I took Henry in our arms and held on to him. There wasn't much for us to say. He'd been booted from his house for being who he is.

What do you say to that?

THE THREE of us fell asleep and didn't wake up until about two in the morning. I went downstairs and made a whole slew of PBJs and brought them back. We sat on my bed and ate in silence.

Finally I asked the question of the night. "So what are you going to do?"

Henry was calm at that point, and after shrugging, he said, "I haven't got a clue."

"You can stay here with me, you know," I offered. "My parents probably wouldn't even notice."

"Maybe. I don't know yet."

"You aren't thinking of trying to act like—*and live like*—you're straight, are you?" Danny dared to ask. I really wanted to know the answer, though, so I waited.

"I don't think they'd believe me at this point if I told them I was straight," Henry told us.

I wasn't satisfied with his answer. "Well, at least you know you're not out on the street," I offered. "How did they find out about us?"

Henry said, "Coach Ruiz saw us three holding hands at lunch, and since he goes to the same church, he called my father and told him. When I got back from basketball, Mom and Dad were waiting for me to come home so they could kick me out."

I took the plates and put them on the bedside table, and, still dressed, we lay back down, pulled the covers up, and held on to Henry. He was more in shock than he was sad. Sometimes there are no words for a situation, so we just touched his hair and rubbed his arms and legs and hugged him—pretty much nonstop.

I wanted to say that I loved them, and I had to bite my tongue to stop myself because I thought it wasn't the right time.

"I'm not gonna go to school tomorrow, you guys. I just need a day to figure things out." Henry sounded weary. I couldn't blame him.

I said the only thing I could think of. "You can stay here. No worries at all. Okay?"

"Thanks, Brody. And thanks for coming over so fast, Danny" was the last thing Henry said before he closed his eyes.

We hugged him one more time and went to sleep.

Free Verse Poetry by Danny D

"Leaves OF Green"
Greenest leaves so like crisp bills,
I pay the price.
Hiking bold up steepest hills
To keep this prize.

In treetops I swing, I sway,
Filling my pockets with greenest leaves,
To meet the oath that I must pay.
I'll pay the price and set him free.

For love I grieve,
A love now lost.
The greenest leaves,
We share the cost.

Henry: My life

IT'S SNOWING when I wake up—the first snow of the season. But it's light snow, not the kind that gets school canceled. So I'm alone. Danny and Brody have been at school for a few hours already.

Brody left me a note on the back of one of the paper plates from last night's PBJ supper.

Here are the keys to the Jeep. I borrowed my mother's Volvo, so I don't need it. Use it to go wherever you need to. I also left some cash so you can grab breakfast and lunch. No worries. It will all turn out fine.

See you after school.

Love,

Brody

I stare at the word *love* and wonder if he means it. Then I climb off the bed, and when I get to my feet, the throbbing in my head stuns me. I make a run for Brody's bathroom, not sure which need is stronger—to piss or barf. I end up throwing up into the toilet.

I take a piss and rinse out my mouth. Then I straighten my clothes, grab my untouched backpack, and head out of Brody's suite without the keys to the Jeep in my hands. I drag my ass to the street in front of his house and start to walk.

I head home.

Brody's notebook

TUESDAY, JANUARY 6
The Welcome to Hell Times
When I got home, Henry was gone. He didn't take my Jeep. He didn't leave a note. He was just gone. I had a very bad feeling.

I drove over to the Food Pyramid, where I'd dropped off Danny fifteen minutes before. He was just emerging from the men's room, dressed in his preppy red polo and neat tan pants.

He looked at me and knew. "Henry's gone, isn't he?"

I nodded. "I'm not sure what happens next," I said.

And Danny said something really smart. "I guess that's up to Henry." He opened his arms to me, and I pretty much dove in. It was a much-needed hug and made me feel better, considering it was given with two arms, not four.

"I'll pick you up for school in the morning?"

He nodded. Sometimes words just suck and all you can do is shrug and nod and shake your head to get your point across. I didn't say goodbye when I walked out of the restaurant. But then, neither did Henry when he walked out of our lives.

CHAPTER 13
ALONE AGAIN.... NATURALLY

Free Verse Poetry by Danny D

"Better"
It took me by surprise
That we, by three, divide.
At first, one part was gone.
As two, we can't stand strong.
As lightning strikes a tree,
The bolt split us in three.
I'm splintered and I'm broke—
A burnt and withered oak.
It's to the forest floor I'll fall,
Or place survival above all.
From them I learned my worth.
So this tree has rebirth
To sway in wind with grace,
To move in steady pace.
My forever's color changed,
As we three are estranged.
But my roots sink in the floor.
They're stronger than before.

Brody's notebook

WEDNESDAY, JANUARY 7
~~*Memoirs of a Slippery Slope Down to Desperation*~~

IT COULD HAPPEN

Maybe this title is dramatic, but I have a strong feeling this is where I'm headed.

Henry didn't come to school today. I was bitterly disappointed, but not at all surprised. He even missed a home basketball game, which is very un-Henry. At lunch I expected Danny to fall apart, but he held himself together admirably. I think I managed to convince him that I was keeping my act together too, but it was truly just an act.

We didn't hold hands like a couple. It seemed like the wrong thing to do.

When I got home, I called Henry's cell phone about ten times. It kept ringing and ringing but never went to voicemail. Then I texted him ten requests to please call, and I even sent him an email. I would have tried to contact him on Facebook, Twitter, and Instagram, but he's not allowed to be on social media.

I remember how freaked out Henry was when Danny tried to bail out on us last fall. That memory doesn't serve any purpose, though, because Danny came back.

I'm done writing in my *Memoirs of a Slippery Slope Down to Desperation*.

I haven't gone running in the snow yet this season. My favorite place to race through the snow is on Main Street. One false move, and I'm in traffic.

Sounds like a plan.

Henry: My life

I HAVE a lot to get caught up on this week. The note in my hand asks that I be excused from missing school last week because I had the flu. It was a lie, and Mom never lies, but she justified it by saying that I had a serious *morality-code* flu. So I walk the straight and narrow path into the school, pretty much literally. At least the straight part.

"Hi, Henry," Jamie Carson greets me at the entrance to the school, as planned.

"Hey, Carson." His family also belongs to the Creator's Bible Church, though you'd never know it from his un-Christ-like behavior when he deals with the more defenseless kids at school. But he's been prepped fully by both of our parents over the course of the weekend on his role in saving me. For some reason he's more than willing to help me out.

"First day of the rest of your life, right, dude?" He runs his hand through his shaggy red hair and grins.

"That's what they say," I reply. I say the right words but can't fake enthusiasm. The right words will have to do.

Jamie is on the basketball team with me. He's the starting point guard and has great ball control. Now he has control of me. He'll be reporting to his parents—who have promised to be in close communication with my parents—on my progress in walking the straight and narrow.

We have a lot of the same classes, so the plan is for us to stick close together. It's not a problem for Jamie, because he's under the impression that when I took Brody and Danny's hands in mine, I was just faking being part of a male threesome to fuck with Lionel Wagner's sanity. He just thinks my parents want the messing around to stop so I can focus on my grades and my sports and my future. And salvation.

We head down the hall to homeroom. Thankfully Danny and Brody aren't there. I'm not ready to face them.

I see a flash of head-to-toe black turn the corner in the hall ahead of me. I know it's Danny. I stiffen my shoulders because my locker is in the same direction, and I remind myself that I'm doing what has to be done if I want a family and a home.

I DREAD lunchtime, but I get my food and head straight to Jamie at the Jocks"R"Us lunch table—my new noontime home. Even though I don't look at them, I can feel Danny and Brody staring at me. If I allow myself to care, I'll be an orphan. Not a fucking option at this point in my life.

Shit.

I pray silently that Lionel will not dish out a serving of crap to Danny and Brody. I don't know if I'm strong enough to go along with that kind of cruelty toward the two guys I love. I take a bite of my turkey sandwich. It has no taste.

Luckily it doesn't come to that because Danny gets up and runs out of the cafeteria. Brody follows closely behind him.

I think maybe I broke them, which wasn't my goal. All I wanted was to save myself.

"Look at the little girls skip away, huh?" No-neck Nelson takes the lead. Everybody at our table laughs.

Except me. I keep chewing.

Brody's notebook

WEDNESDAY, JANUARY 21
   ~~*The Final Chapter*~~
   I think it's really over.
   I don't know why I bother to keep this diary any longer.
   Its purpose was to document the growth of our relationship. And with Danny, Henry, and me, it was a threesome or bust. Two of us won't work. So it's over.
   I'm left with the bad habit of keeping a dang diary.
   And I have a feeling—it's a bad feeling. Why can't I ever have a good feeling?
   I have a bad feeling that there never was an "us," because if it had been real, it wouldn't have blown away with a single harsh gust of wind.

Lunch block B is symbolic of our ruin:

Henry has joined forces with the jocks. He *is* a jock, so it makes complete sense. And he seems happy enough, which is good. He hasn't looked at me once since the last night he slept in my bed—tucked between Danny and me—the day before he refused the offer

145

of my Jeep keys. Henry had no interest in taking the Jeep for a final joyride. I respect him for that.

Danny has taken to eating upstairs with the artsy crowd. For all I know, he has his eye on Mr. Lansing. Mr. Lansing is middle-aged, kind of cute, and likely even gay. He's nuts about Danny, if not way too old for him, but that's par for the course in Danny's life. He's better than most of Danny's boyfriends who came before.

As for me, I eat alone.

It's okay. I'm a loner, really.

It's cool.

And I write this without any bitterness, which is hard to believe, but it's also true. I'm returning to my natural state, after an almost four-year break. High school was a pleasant interlude of connection in a life I'm meant to spend without anyone to answer to.

LOL. "Pleasant interlude" makes pain sound so inviting.

But it's all good. I like being alone.

Time to stop being so dramatic.

There are so many important things I've long neglected to do. I'm ready to get started.

Brody's notebook

THURSDAY, JANUARY 29

I had a talk with Danny today. But in the end, nothing changed. It was as over between us after the talk as it was before. I'm cool with that.

"I'm not gonna need rides to school after today, Brody." That was how he started and how everything ended, I guess. Danny climbed into my Jeep, buckled in because he knows I won't drive until I hear the click, and told me he didn't need me anymore.

All that was left to our relationship were those ten-minute drives to school every morning. And there he sat, telling me he no longer needed them. "My mom just got a job working at Cullfield General

Hospital in the sanitation department. She has to be there at seven, so she offered to drop me off at school on her way." He shrugged and looked out the passenger-side window. "Mom's been telling me she wants to spend more time with me, so I figure, why not?"

Since Christina's breakup with her Boston boyfriend, she's been trying to straighten up her act. Danny thinks the amount of heavy drinking they did together down in the city might have scared her. So she quit her job at the convenience store, found a new job with benefits, and according to Danny, has been going to AA and acting like more of a mom to him.

Which is all well and good, but the final scrap of a bond between Danny and me just vanished. "That's cool," I replied, and I wondered just how fast I'd have to go around a hairpin turn to make my Jeep drive on two wheels but not flip over.

"You talked to Henry at all lately?" He asked as he continued to stare out the window.

"Nope. I haven't heard a word from him."

"He's an asshole. I should've known," Danny said, and then he yawned, as though to prove to me he didn't care too much.

I experienced a momentary urge to defend Henry. For a split second, the hair stood up on the back of my neck with the certain knowledge that Henry isn't an asshole at all, but the feeling passed quickly.

Then out of the blue, Danny said, "I told Mom about what happened to me in the bathroom of the art wing."

"No way. You did?"

"Well, you used to be after me all the time to get some justice for some of the bad shit that's been done to me." He was right about that. "And I never did anything about Jared, which I should have, so I figured I'd tell Mom about the swirlie thing, just to see what she thought."

"And? What did she think?" I asked.

"Jesus. I never saw her that mad. She's talking to Principal Marcotte sometime this week." Danny seemed sort of surprised that his mother was so angry on his behalf.

And I was floored to learn that Danny turned to his mother about the bullying at school. "I'm glad, Danny." I meant it.

"So maybe we can grab dinner this weekend," Danny suggested when I parked the Jeep in front of the high school.

"Sure," I replied.

Danny jumped out, ran off toward the school, and shouted, "I'll text you."

"I won't hold my breath," I answered, but he was too far away to hear.

Brody's notebook

SUNDAY, FEBRUARY 1
No word from Danny all weekend. Not a surprise. Not much could surprise me now, I don't think. So it's Sunday afternoon, and I have a few more hours to kill until it's time to go to sleep.

When I was sitting on my bed a little while ago, looking out my window into the backyard, I had to fight the craziest urge. I had an overwhelming impulse to stand up, walk over to the window, open it, and take a flying leap.

I'd try to make it a safe leap because, despite the risks I take, I never *intentionally* hurt myself. I'd bend my knees slightly, but wouldn't lock them, and I'd stay loose and relaxed. Then I'd drop out the window, descend the three stories, and roll when my feet hit the ground.

I pushed this idea to the back of my mind. It could always serve as a possible Plan B if I can't find anything else to do this afternoon.

Brody's notebook

STILL SUNDAY, February 1
~~*The Day That Wouldn't End*~~
Why are there no bulls in Cullfield?

I could have so much fun with bulls. I could make them mad and then try to fight them or ride them or run with them. Hell, I could even tip them over. But no, there isn't a single bull in this dang town.

Henry: My life

LUNCH BLOCK B is still the hardest part of my day, and it has been since about a week after Danny, Brody, and I went our separate ways. Strangely it's also the highlight of my day. I'm surrounded by the cool people—the ones who matter in school. We crack jokes and laugh really loud. Some of them strategically pick on weak kids and even vulnerable teachers in the caf. Then we laugh even louder.

I never join in with that bullshit, although I admit to smiling and chuckling a little when everybody else is laughing. I kind of have to if I don't want to stick out like a sore thumb. Thankfully the people who matter have forgotten all about the day I held hands with Danny and Brody, one lunch table to the right of where I sit right now. It's like that never happened.

I look over at Brody, who sits alone every day at lunch. He has the entire "Island of Misfit Toys" lunch table to himself. Danny must be eating lunch upstairs in the art lounge. I don't have a clue. In fact, I haven't seen him in ages. Maybe he quit school.

Brody and I catch eyes. It happens once during every lunch block B. And I'm the one who makes it happen. I stare at him until he looks my way. It's my only connection to those guys, and it makes my eyes burn every time, but I do it anyway. Brody always smiles when our gazes meet. At first it was a hopeful smile, now it's just a pleasant one. He's not an asshole, even to the guy who fucked him over.

I miss them so badly. I miss my old friends. I miss having *real* friends. I miss what was growing between us.

"So you up for a party tonight at Brent's house, Perkins? Amanda Ortega is gonna be there, and she has it bad for you." My new pal Lionel elbows me and grins. Since I gave up my standards in life, Wagner hasn't had a problem with me at all.

I nod at Brody, look back toward my new friend, and reply, "Sure. Why the fuck not?" I really don't give a shit what I do with my free time. It's not like I have to break my ass studying or volunteering anymore. I've submitted all my college applications, and all I have to do is see if my mother *or* my father wins the battle that determines if I go D1 or divinity. One of the schools I applied to is D1 *and* Christian. If I get in there, I can make *both* of their days.

"I'll come get you at eight."

"Sounds like a plan, Wagner."

Brody's notebook

WEDNESDAY, MARCH 18

~~My Found and Lost Journal~~

Time flies when you're having fun, which means that when life sucks, time drags on and on.

I hardly ever write in this notebook these days because what's the point? Nothing ever happens anymore.

Nothing that matters happens, at least. I get up every day and go to school. Maybe I go to a club once in a while because, even though I don't officially belong, some of them actually depend on me. And then I go out and find something stupid to do to get my mind off missing what I had, which somehow got tossed into the trash. Only then can I sleep.

I *should* go out and make new friends, but that seems pointless. It's March of senior year. I'll be leaving in less than three months. That isn't enough time to make friends that matter.

IT COULD HAPPEN

I've reconsidered going to college, or at least going directly after high school. I think I'd rather take a gap year... do some traveling. There are a few stellar adrenaline rushes I want to get—a zip line in the UK that hits 100 mph, a 108-story free-fall tower in Vegas, and then there's always storm chasing.

CHAPTER 14
ROCK BOTTOM

Brody's notebook

WEDNESDAY, APRIL 1
~~*Fuck This Journal*~~
There's nothing like an April 1st blizzard. School's cancelled, and everything.

When Mom called to me up the stairs this morning, "No school today, Little Brody," at first I didn't believe her.

I yelled back, "This is an April Fool's Day prank, right?"

"Look out the window," Dad yelled and added, "We had to miss our aqua-aerobics class because of the condition of the roads."

"Oh no. Not that." My reply was sarcastic, and I immediately regretted it. So I chirped in a sweet voice, "Thanks for the info," just to make up for it. I don't make a very good asshole, no matter how I try.

I opened my eyes, looked out the window, and saw the snow swirling. The ground was white, and when I closed my eyes, I could hear the wind wreaking havoc on the roof.

I've been waiting for a day like this for forever, it seems. This winter was so mild it didn't even feel like winter—an inch of snow here, two inches there. And finally a real snowstorm.

MOM AND Dad are nagging me to build a snowman with them, which is kind of cute, even if it's lame. But I lied and told them I have to drive Danny to work. For the record I haven't talked to Danny in a week and I have no clue if he's working.

But I have plans for today. Big plans.

Henry: My life

I'M STILL lying in bed when I get the phone call. I look at the clock on my phone before I answer and see that it's noon.

Nothing like sleeping the day away.

Depressed much, Henry?

"Hello?" I don't recognize the number.

"Hello, is this Henry Perkins?"

"Uh… yeah. This is Henry."

"This is Brody's mother, Dottie Decker. I'm sorry to disturb you, but I wondered if you had seen or heard from Brody today." She sounds worried, which is unusual for her because she never before had much concern where Brody was or what he was doing.

"I'm sorry, Mrs. Decker. I haven't seen him. And he hasn't called me either."

"Well, he can't call you on his cell phone, seeing as he left it on his bed."

That's odd. Brody's phone was always attached to him, in case Danny or I needed him. "Where did he say he was going?" I glance out the window. "It looks really bad out there."

"Yes, dear. That's why I'm calling. He left at about eight thirty this morning to drive Danny to work. And he never came home."

"Did you call Danny to see if he got there?" My heart starts to pound. My palms are sticky too.

I'm not supposed to care about Brody. *I'm not allowed to care.*

"Yes, and Danny said he hasn't spoken to Brody in a week."

Oh God. Something's wrong.

"Bernie and I are going to take a ride around and see if we can find him." She is not just worried. Mrs. Decker is distraught. I'm surprised that she cares so much. It must be serious.

153

"Be careful, and I hope you find him, ma'am. Please let me know when you do."

She doesn't say goodbye.

And I don't put my cell phone down. I immediately call Danny.

"What the fuck do *you* want?" This is Danny's greeting to me, which I richly deserve.

"We need to find Brody. I'm worried about him."

"As if *you* give a flying shit about Brody. And as if *I* give a shit about what you're worried about." His voice has a sharp edge. Sharp as in, it could easily slice through a piece of paper.

"Please, Danny. Let me come over and talk to you."

"Jesus." There's a long silence on the other end and then an equally long sigh. "All right. You can come over, but *only* for Brody's sake."

He also ends the call without a goodbye—the second call in a row that ended that way. Again I acknowledge how deserving I am of that treatment.

I use the bathroom and then put on the warmest clothes I can find in my room, which end up being jeans, a T-shirt, a sweatshirt, and my letter jacket. I can't find any gloves, but I don't waste time searching for them. I run down the hall and find Mom in the kitchen.

"Mom, I need to use the car."

"I don't think so, Henry. The roads are too slippery."

I don't even hesitate when it comes to lying to her. It's easy. I've been lying to my parents for so long. "But Amanda called me, and said she's stranded at the gym. She needs a ride, Mom, and I really want to help her out. I promise I'll be careful." I smile at her sheepishly, as if Amanda Ortega means something to me.

"Oh, Henry. You're such a gentleman, helping out a young lady in need. You can use the minivan, but please be careful." She walks to the hook on the wall and pulls the keys off.

I grab them and then put on my old high-tops. "I might spend some time with Amanda at her house, okay?" I need to buy some time to find Brody.

Mom smiles at me in *that* way. "Oh, Henry… you have a girlfriend. Why didn't you tell me?"

I don't stick around long enough to answer.

DANNY MARCHES out the front door of his apartment building the second I step onto the snowy walkway. I turn around and follow him back to the minivan that I left running on the road. We get in, and Danny stares straight ahead.

"We've gotten about six inches already," I tell him. "And the wind is picking up."

"Thanks for the update, Mr. Weatherman. Now let's figure out where the hell Brody is."

My stomach does a somersault. I'm out of my league. Brody was always the one to guide us through the shit. "Well, first let's find a place I can park, and we can talk."

"Go to Cullfield Pizza. They always keep their lot plowed."

We drive there in silence. But what is there to say? The only thing we have in common is that we both want to find Brody.

Once I park I ask, "Do you think Brody would go to Branton Beach? He was really into it during that hurricane."

Danny turns in the passenger seat so he can look my way, but not at me. "Yeah, he could be there. He loves the wind."

"Remember he went to that hill on the night of the really bad lightning storm last summer?"

"Pierce Hill. That's another place he could be." Danny smiles, probably thinking about Brody. "He told me he almost got struck by lightning that night."

"He's reckless."

"He always has been. It's like he has a death wish or something."

For the first time, we look each other straight in the eyes. It's been so long. We both shudder, and my eyes begin to burn and fill.

"Don't you dare fuckin' cry, Perkins. This whole thing is your fault. If he dies today, it's all on you."

155

He's 100 percent right. And I can't stop the tears, but neither can Danny. "I had to leave you guys... I *had* to...." It feels good to let it all go.

"You didn't even tell us why. You just disappeared one day. Even my friggin' mother used to say goodbye when she took off on me." Danny, usually stoic and unaffected, is wrecked, because I wrecked him.

"I'm sorry. But do you think I *wanted* to leave you guys? Being with you and Brody was my idea of heaven. I didn't *want* to go anywhere."

We cry like a couple of damned babies until Danny takes a deep breath and says, "I trusted you, Henry. And so did Brody."

"I know. I know you guys did." I rub my face hard with my palms. And then I admit the truth. "I was afraid to lose my family."

Danny grabs my hand and squeezes. It isn't gentle at all. "*We* were your family."

Again he's right. I wish I could go back in time and change what I did. "Let's find Brody and have this talk with him too." Danny nods but hangs on to my hand. I feel like one foot is back in the doorway of my true home.

"Remember when he took us to Butternut Mountain? And we ate our sandwiches out on the ledge?" Danny asks, his voice suddenly shaky.

"Oh shit," I say. I remember, and I know exactly why Danny brought it up. "He said he wanted to go onto that ledge if there was ever a blizzard."

"To see the snow swirling and.... Henry, we have to get there. He could fall off or freeze or...."

I quickly pull out of the parking lot. If the pavement weren't covered with snow, I would have burned rubber in true Brody style, for sure. It takes a while to drive to Butternut Mountain, thanks to the snow, but we get our reward when we arrive.

"Brody's Jeep. It's over there. He's here," Danny says. He doesn't sound surprised.

Brody's Jeep is parked at a hasty angle on the shoulder of the road. Danny and I jump out of the van, and we head for the trail. Neither of us is dressed for a blizzard, but we don't let that stop us. And climbing the trail is ten times harder in the snow. I help Danny through the places where snow has filled in crevices. When we get to the top, we're in whiteout conditions. I hold on to Danny's hand, and we take tiny steps as we head toward the ledge. I'm very aware that if we make one false move, we're goners.

"Brody," Danny calls, but it seems like his voice is sucked into a wintery vacuum. "Brody, we're here. We're here for you."

I yell too. "Decker! Don't move. We'll come get you. Just shout to let us know where you are."

All we can hear is gusting wind. But when we make our way to the place where the rock juts out a few feet beyond the ledge, we catch a glimpse of Brody through the blinding snow. He's stretched out flat and is very still. Suddenly I'm scared. And I'm quite certain that I made a huge mistake when I left those guys. Because somebody who doesn't give a shit wouldn't feel as wigged out with worry and guilt and regret as I do.

"Danny, I'm gonna go out there and get him. I need you to help us off the edge. Okay?"

Danny nods. "Don't let him slip. And don't *you* slip either. Jesus."

Taking small steady steps, I make my way to the still body on the protruding ledge. I kneel down beside him and see that his eyes are open. He's watching the snow swirl in the air. His eyelashes are caked with ice. "Brody, it's time to go home." I say it so he can hear me over the wind, but I use a gentle tone.

He pulls my face down so his frozen lips are against my ear. "I knew you'd come," he says in a weak and shaky voice. Then he closes his eyes.

"Brody…. Brody." I grab him by the shoulders and shake, scared shitless that he froze to death and died right in front of me. But his eyes flutter and open. "Listen, Decker, I need you to help me get you down off this mountain."

Brody smiles just a little bit and nods once. But he doesn't make a move to get up.

So I try another angle. "Me and Danny aren't gonna leave here without you, dude. If that means freezing to death, then we're all in this together."

He finally shakes his head. "Perky, you need to take Danny home."

"I'm gonna take *both* of you home," I insist and lift him so he's sitting. "Are you gonna help me?"

"I'll help." He attempts to get to his feet, but slips to the side, which makes me gasp. His feet are probably frozen and he can't control his movements.

Thanks to the high wind and the whipping snow, I can't see how far the drop is beneath the ledge. But I don't need to see it. We're dead if we fall, and that's the long and short of it. "Let's crawl instead."

We turn onto our bellies and army crawl toward Danny. When we finally get off the rock that juts out into the sky, Danny grasps Brody's hands and helps him to stand. Once I'm on my feet too, we begin the long trip down the mountain.

We're all mostly frozen when we finally get to the bottom. I suggest, "Let's leave Brody's Jeep here and drive back to his house in my van."

Danny agrees, and they get into the backseat, where Brody promptly falls asleep with his head on Danny's lap. I blast the heat and drive us home.

ONCE MR. and Mrs. Decker have recovered from their relief that Brody is home in one piece, we go upstairs to Brody's suite. We strip off our soaking wet clothes and dig through Brody's drawers until we find stuff to wear that comes close to fitting us. Brody slides between his sheets in just a pair of sweatpants. He hasn't stopped shaking.

"C-could you p-pile another blanket or two from the corner on top of m-me?" he asks as though we haven't been apart for almost three months.

I do as he requests and then wait for him to ask me what the hell I'm doing at his house. But he turns away from Danny and me and closes his eyes.

"We need to talk," I say to him. And then I admit the truth. "*I* need to talk."

"I wanted to talk in January and in February and in March." He yawns. "I wanted to talk yesterday, when you were staring at me in the cafeteria."

"Point taken," I mumble. He owes me nothing, just as Danny owes me nothing.

Within a minute Brody's asleep.

Danny comes to my side and places a hand on my arm. I cover his hand with mine and squeeze. Again I feel like part of me has come home. But not all of me.

"I need to bring the minivan back to my house," I tell him.

Danny looks up at me, obviously worried.

"I'm gonna come back here after I pick up a few things from my room. I swear."

"You're gonna leave your home?"

I nod. "I can't change what I did before. And maybe you and Brody can't forgive me. But at least I can be true to myself."

Danny sits down on the edge of the bed and runs his hand through Brody's drooping blond spikes. "What do you mean?"

I take a few steps toward the bedroom door. "I'm not really losing much if I lose people who can't love and accept me for who I am."

"Yeah. But still, it'll be hard to walk away from your mom and dad."

"Not as hard as living with the lies."

"I'm coming with you."

"No. Stay here with Brody. He needs you."

"You need me too, Henry."

"That's true. But still, stay with Brody. I have to do this on my own."

Danny nods and says, "If you need to, you can live with me until we go to college. Mom won't care as long as we don't make too much noise."

Once again my eyes burn. "Thanks, Danny. I might take you up on that," I say, and I head off to do what I should have done in January.

I'M NOT scared at all. My mouth isn't dry. My stomach is staying in its correct, upright position, and there's no throbbing in my temples. I'm just doing what I need to do so I can be my own man.

I park the minivan in the driveway and come in through the side door. Without a sound I go down the hall and grab the biggest duffle bag out of the hall closet. In my room I stuff it with as many clothes and sneakers as I can fit. I fill my backpack with books and my computer, and then, with bags in hand, I head to the kitchen. Mom and Dad are making salad.

"Why the duffle bag, son?" Dad asks. He's not alarmed, just curious. He's so convinced that I wouldn't dare to step out of line.

"I'm moving out."

Dad laughs. He thinks I'm joking.

But Mom looks up and fixes her eyes on me. "What on earth are you talking about, Henry?"

Here goes nothing. "I'm gay. And as a gay man, I'm not welcome in this house."

Dad drops the knife in his hand onto the chopping board. "We've been through this already, Henry. You are *not* gay. You were just confused."

"And you spent the day with Amanda," Mom counters. "Your girlfriend…."

I shake my head. "Nope. I'm gay. And I won't force you to look at me any longer. If you need me, I'll probably be staying with Danny Denisco." I place my cell phone on the counter.

I head back out into the snow with the heavy duffle bag on one arm and my backpack over my other shoulder—and no future connection to my family by birth.

CHAPTER 15
NOWHERE TO GO BUT UP

Henry: My life

THE SNOW is winding down by the time I get back to Brody's house. I'm cold and wet from the long walk, but I somehow feel warm and light inside. When I come upstairs, Danny and Brody are sitting in the little living room in his suite, eating bowls of chicken noodle soup. There's a bowl for me.

I sit down, take the tin foil off the top, and lift my spoon. Before I start to eat, I say, "Don't worry, Brody. I'm not going to force my presence on you. Danny said I could stay with him."

"That would be the easy way out, wouldn't it? Eat my soup and then take off with Danny," Brody says, but he's otherwise focused on the bowl in his lap.

We eat in silence until Danny gets up to collect the bowls. I try again. "I've made a huge mess of things with you guys." I take a deep breath and act like the man I want to be. "I can't tell you how sorry I am. I was scared, and I made a huge mistake."

I now have Brody and Danny's full attention.

"I just want you to know that I love you guys."

Danny's eyes begin to fill, as they had earlier, but I don't cry. I just look from Danny to Brody and live with my regret.

"Come sit down with me, both of you," Brody says softly.

Danny and I sit on either side of him on the couch.

"First, thanks for rescuing me off the mountain. I probably would have… well, you know. I think you guys saved my life." Brody looks from me to Danny. His expression is sincere.

He can't be thanking *me*. It isn't right. "But I put you there. I put you on that ledge, bro," I insist.

"You didn't put me there, Perky. And neither did you, Danny." Brody shakes his head. "I don't know if you guys have noticed, but I have certain tendencies toward, you know… toward reckless behavior."

"Those tendencies would be hard to miss," Danny admits with a short laugh.

"I want to go back in time to where we were before it all fell apart, but I know we need to find a totally new path," Brody explains, but it only confuses me.

"So where do we go from here?" I ask.

"How about to Prospect University?" Brody eliminates my confusion with his simple response.

I can't *not* smile when I say, "We have until May to commit."

Danny nods. "I'm in."

Fixing everything I screwed up can't be that easy. "We have a lot to talk about. And I have so much to make up to you guys."

Brody shakes his head and glances at Danny. "I don't require a heart-to-heart with Henry, if you don't, Danny." Brody has always shied away from gut spilling, but *he* isn't halfway out the door, racing away from his feelings either.

"Henry and I already talked about stuff. I think we're cool."

"You're both here. That says it all to me."

"And you aren't frozen on a snowy ledge," I add. "I think we can call that a major success."

Brody gets up and, right in front of the bed, he pulls off all his clothes. "We need to share our body heat." He looks from Danny to me. "Time to strip down, boys."

"Set the alarm so we get up on time in the morning. We can't miss school," Danny instructs me.

"When did you turn into Mr. Punctuality?" I ask, again feeling at a loss.

"When I committed to go to Prospect U. It's already a done deal for me," Danny tells us. "Literally."

Both of my guys stand naked beside the bed. They look good, but I'm not sure how much of them I can have. I've been gone so long.

"I'll take the middle," Brody announces, and he climbs in and places himself strategically in the center of the big bed. He's followed by Danny. I'm last to take off my clothes. I have a very interested audience too. Eyes on me, Danny groans, and Brody holds his arms open. I take a second to thank the God I know is there for me that I'm back.

I turn off the light on the bedside table, slide onto the edge of the bed, and slip under the covers. The sensation of being home overwhelms me. Danny and I turn toward Brody, and our hands find one another. It's bizarre, but we start by touching one another's faces—not kissing—just running our fingers over one another's lips and eyes and chins. We work our way down to necks and chests, and from there the exploration turns into making love with our hands.

Still watching and not kissing, we latch on to one another's dicks and begin to pull. It feels as if we were never apart.

"Do you forgive me?" I'm close to my big finish too soon, but I have to ask.

"We *love* you," Brody murmurs, closes his eyes, and just like that, he lets go.

"Can we not ever do that again?" Danny asks, and when I nod, he fills my hand.

I know he means, can we never break up again, and I say, "Once is way more than enough. I love you guys too." It ends up taking another full minute for me to get there because my head is still churning with regret. But when it's my turn, I give up my guilt as I let go.

WE TAKE turns cleaning up in the bathroom. When we're settled back in bed, Brody asks me, "So you left home for real?"

"Yeah. I really did. I might have to beg off of you guys until I get to Prospect U. I have no cash, and I'm basically homeless."

"Not a problem at all," Brody says, and I can tell that he's smiling. "Leaving home took balls, Perky. Seriously."

"It was easier than you might think," I reply.

"They're always looking for busboys at the Food Pyramid. You can get a summer job there with me," Danny's says, changing the subject. His hand is draped across Brody's waist and his fingers play on my chest.

"I'll apply this weekend. I can start as soon as track is over."

It's quiet until Brody declares, "I guess I'll cancel my plans to take a selfie with a moving train, you know, now that you guys are back in the picture."

I can feel the vibration as Danny kicks Brody's shin. "Jesus, Brody. Don't be a dipshit."

Free Verse Poetry by Danny D

"The good stuff"
waking up between them
touching without thinking
laughing about nothing
holding hands in public
planning nights together
believing it can happen
trusting it won't end

Henry: My life

IT ISN'T as simple as "I think I'll move into Brody's suite," and I just cart my stuff in.

So this morning Brody and I sit down with Mr. and Mrs. Decker to have a friendly chat. Danny has come to the "family meeting" too, and my guys sit on either side of me on the big leather couch in the Deckers' living room.

I'm awkward as hell, because, in one sense, I'm truly alone in life. I really have no family anymore.

"So, Henry, Brody told us your parents asked that you leave home?" Mr. Decker asks, shaking his head. I hope his disappointment isn't directed at me.

Before I have a chance to answer, Mrs. Decker serves me a cup of tea in a tiny flowery cup. "This is lemon ginger tea from the Town Tea Shak on the Cullfield rotary. It will boost your immune system, dear."

"Thank you, ma'am," I reply.

She smiles at me broadly as she continues to pour and pass out cups of tea.

"And yes, Mr. Decker, my parents told me they didn't want me to live with them anymore."

"You can tell them why, Perky. My parents are cool," Brody announces, and I feel my face get hot.

Brody never says too much about his parents to Danny and me. They always seem to be *way* in the background of his life. But he smiles at them as though he knows that, underneath the distance between them, they've got his back. And I want to explain, but I'm scared to be tossed out again.

"You're probably freaking out at this point, so *I'll* tell them." Brody slides over so he's right next to me and puts his arm around my shoulders. "Henry's parents asked him to leave because he's gay."

"And you, Little Brody, are Henry's boyfriend?" Mr. Perkins asks. I watch his face very carefully for signs of a frown, but there are none.

Brody immediately jumps in. "Call me Brody, Dad. Just Brody."

Little Brody? That's kind of cute. I push the thought to the back of my mind. I've got more pressing shit to deal with.

"And yes to your question. Henry *and* Danny and I are in a… we're in a serious relationship." He stumbles as he searches for the right words, not because he's scared.

I have trouble getting a good breath as I wait for the Deckers' reaction. Danny seems to have the same problem. Most people would think what we're doing together is stepping over the line. We reach out and grab one another's hands.

Finally Mr. Decker speaks. "Well, as I always say, you only have one life and you need to live it as you see fit." Then he smiles, and it's a real smile.

Mrs. Decker sits down on the chair opposite her husband. "None of you are drinking your tea," she says with a pout and folds her arms across her chest, insulted.

The three of us on the couch obediently lift our teacups and take a united sip. But I can't believe she's thinking about tea when my life is on the line.

"It's very good tea, Mrs. Decker." Danny is genuinely impressed. "What kind did you say it was?"

Huh?

Mrs. Decker gets up, goes into the kitchen, and comes back with a round tin in her hands. "Here, dear." She passes it to Danny. "My gift to you. It's available at the Town Tea Shak if you become addicted, as I have."

"Thank you, Mrs. Decker. I think I owe you a few lemon poppy seed muffins from the restaurant *I* work at."

Mrs. Decker licks her lips. "A poppy seed muffin sounds delicious right about now."

I'm having trouble believing that we just told Brody's parents we're a gay threesome, and the resulting discussion is centered on ginger tea and poppy seed muffins.

Brody brings us back. "Mom, Dad, Henry needs a place to stay until we head off to college, and I want to know if he can stay here."

"I don't see why that would be a problem. You're eighteen, right?" I can't believe Mr. Decker acts like it's just any other day in his life. *Didn't he hear us say we're gay and we're all dating one another?*

I nod. "Yes, sir."

"Then you're more than welcome to stay here, Henry. And Danny, you're welcome to come over whenever you'd like." He glances at his wife. "Dottie, it looks like you have four boys, including me, to feed this summer."

"I fed more boys than that when the kids were growing up, Bernie. It'll be easy."

Brody pats my back and smiles as though that's the best news so far. "Thanks, Mom. This is going to be great."

Helping me out with my life's biggest tragedy seems to be an opportunity for his family to bond. I'm floored.

"Do we need to let the high school know Henry is going to be staying here?" Mr. Perkins asks Brody.

"Henry and I will go to the office and tell them this week," Brody replies.

"Well, then, this is settled. Bernie, I think we need to make a trip to the grocery store." Brody's mother gets up, looks around, and mumbles about where she left her purse. When she finds it, she announces, "I'm going to go put lipstick on. If you boys want anything special from the store, write it down, and Little Brody, please go get those reusable bags you always nag us to use out of the pantry."

Danny laughs and leans toward me. "*Little Brody*. We're never gonna let him live *that* down."

Brody comes back with about a half-dozen cloth bags and hands them to his father as his parents walk out the door.

When Brody sits back down, I feel thankful, but still a lot like an orphan. And even though we've been apart for a long time, Brody seems to know what I'm thinking. "Take it from Little Brody, we aren't going to let you be alone."

Brody's notebook

TUESDAY, APRIL 21

A Threelationship Worth Fighting For—*yes, it's cheesy, but I'm gonna go with this title today.*

Although my adrenaline rushes have been placed on permanent restriction by my boyfriends, I will admit I got a huge surge of adrenaline the first time the three of us walked into the cafeteria holding hands.

It was daring and scary, and I thought it was going to be very risky. But a few really weird things happened. First, Henry didn't care what anybody thought. He walked in with his head high, and when we sat down, he scooped up one of Danny's hands and one of mine and held them tightly on top of the lunch table.

I asked him, "Aren't you freaking out to hold hands with us in front of Lionel and Jamie and No-neck?"

Henry shrugged but didn't seem to be fazed. "I'm way more afraid to be the dude I was when I hung out with them."

The other strange thing was that, just like at our visit to Prospect University, some kids looked at us—they were curious and maybe they thought we weren't acting normal, whatever that is—but nobody really cared what we were doing.

Wagner said something like, "Isn't it romantic?" when he saw us holding hands, but then he got back to a serious discussion he was having with another kid who's going to the same state university as him.

None of the other jocks seemed too concerned with us at all. In fact most of them were doing some last-minute cramming for their afternoon finals. Maybe it's because Lionel and No-neck ended up getting suspended from school thanks to giving Danny swirlies in the bathroom last fall, and the rest of the jocks don't want to get barred from graduation. Or maybe even these guys are growing up and moving on with their lives. It's April, and all of the seniors are making huge decisions about the future. Harassing three kids at a parallel lunch table probably doesn't captivate them the way it did in September.

Brody's notebook

TUESDAY, MAY 19

It's finals week for seniors, and Danny's mother is letting him stay over at my house so we can have intense study sessions. It feels like a preview of college—the three of us living together in my little suite, studying our butts off, and only going downstairs to Mom's "dining hall" for meals.

And it's epic.

During one study break, while we all stared at our books in the sitting room, Henry brought up a topic I was hoping they'd forgotten about. "We've talked about a lot of shit, Decker, but we haven't talked about your insane need for speed."

Danny nodded in agreement before Henry even finished his sentence. I decided that maybe they'd set me up.

But I also knew it was time to face the music, and I *needed* to face it. I nearly killed all three of us when I went out onto that ledge on Butternut Mountain in the April blizzard. "I'm listening." I decided to let them take the lead.

"No more risking your life," Danny told me. Then he got up from the couch, headed to the sink to get a glass of water, and said, "I'm *so* done with that."

"You're gonna have to figure out a way to get your adrenaline rush that isn't so friggin' dangerous," Henry added. I could tell by the tentative way he said it that he didn't want to lecture me, but at the same time he needed to get his point across.

"You mean you want me to drive slower?" I asked.

"For starters," Danny replied and came over to lie down beside Henry and me on the floor.

"We want you to wear a helmet when you're riding on anything that has wheels." That was Henry's idea. "And yeah, you need to drive more carefully, for everybody's sake."

"And no more swimming during storms of any kind." Danny didn't have to think too hard to come up with that one.

Henry and I closed our books and pushed them out of the way so we could wrap ourselves around one another on the rug. Henry lay flat on his back between Danny and me, who curled around him. "How about this? You can get adrenaline rushes in one of two ways."

"What ways?" I asked.

"By taking ice-cold showers and watching horror movies," Henry told me, and I could tell that he meant it.

"But not too many cold showers," Danny joked. He stretched his leg across Henry's belly and let his foot land directly on my crotch.

"Nice move, Danny," Henry said, and then he leaned down to kiss both of our foreheads.

"So promise us that you're all done with being reckless," Danny ordered and slipped his foot up beneath my shorts.

I gasped and started to make the promise, but Henry cleared his throat. "Brody, we aren't trying to control you or stifle your personality or anything. We're just asking you to be safer when you get your adrenaline rushes," Henry explains. "Like we want you to wear protective gear and not do stuff that could actually kill you."

"That sounds reasonable." I snapped my legs closed and trapped Danny's roving foot. "But if we ever go to Australia…."

Danny and Henry groaned.

"There's this… this *sport*… called crocodile bungee jumping…," I said.

Another groan.

"Ask us again for the green light when we're planning a trip to Australia," Danny said. Then he leaned up to look at Henry. "Remind me to do a little research on safe practices in crocodile bungee jumping."

The temptation to kiss one another was suddenly too great. Henry jumped to his feet and grabbed our hands. "Bed," he said. He didn't have to ask us twice.

Henry and I rushed to the bed and flopped down on our backs next to each other, but we left a narrow space for Danny in the middle. That's how it usually goes—the three of us lying in a row and then leaning toward the guy in the middle to get things going. But instead Danny pulled away from us and knelt at the foot of our bed, between Henry's feet and mine. He looked at me and said, "I think I know something we could do that might distract you from your need for speed, Brody."

"*I* wanna be distracted too," Henry piped up in a cute little kid's voice.

"Chill, Henry. I'd never leave you out of the fun," Danny replied and slowly undid his black button-down shirt. The look in his eyes wasn't particularly dangerous, mostly because he hadn't put on his dark eyeliner, but there was still something distinctly predatory about it. "I've got some *serious* skills you guys have no clue about." He stopped unbuttoning just long enough to rest his hands on our crotches for a second.

Henry and I easily got the message. We both shivered. And neither of us was cold.

"I think *now* is the right moment to show you." He shook his shoulders enough to make the shirt slide off his back and drop onto the floor. I glanced at Henry so we could mutually enjoy the sexy striptease. His eyes looked as wide as mine felt. And when Danny undid his black skinny jeans, he asked, "That cool with you guys?"

I couldn't find my voice, so all I did was nod. Again I looked at Henry. He was nodding too, and drooling a little.

"I suggest that you both strip down below the waist." When he finished unzipping his fly, Danny slid off the edge of the bed and pulled his pants off.

Henry leaned toward me and said, "Shit. He's going commando." As if I hadn't noticed.

We both stared at Danny's small, pale butt as he walked to the bedroom door to check that it was locked. When he turned around, satisfied that we had complete privacy, he rolled his eyes and asked, "Why on earth do you guys still have your shorts on?"

I nudged Henry in the gut to bring him back to earth, and we both tugged hard on our boxers. We succeeded in getting naked in less than a split second without injuring ourselves or each other.

"Move close together." Danny took charge, which hadn't happened in bed before. Like obedient kids, though, we slithered to the side until our bare hips were pressed together, and when Danny climbed back on the bed, he crawled on top of us so he straddled our legs. When he took our dicks in his hands and quickly bent right down over us, I stopped breathing. I'm pretty sure Henry did too, because the room was dead silent.

The anticipation was almost too much.

And the sensation of Danny's soft lips parting and then his warm tongue taking my dick into his mouth brought out something kind of caveman in me. The urge to thrust my entire length between his lips and start pumping was almost unbearable, but somehow I managed to let him go at his own pace. I didn't stop myself from admiring the way Danny's jet-black hair looked draped all over my crotch, though.

"That's a fucking beautiful sight." Henry was watching too.

After a minute or maybe more, Danny pulled his magical lips off my dick and, still bent over me, looked up at Henry. "You think it's beautiful?"

We *both* nodded.

"Then check out how it *feels*." And Danny shifted his attentions to Henry's dick.

"O-o-o-oh, my friggin' word," Henry cried out when Danny took him in his mouth. I moaned too, because I knew how mind-blowing it felt… and because Danny was still stroking my dick.

At one point, as Danny was shifting from Henry to me, he muttered, "I want you guys to suck face, 'stead of just lying there and gawking at me."

It seemed like a reasonable request, so I reached over and turned Henry's head my way. Before I kissed him, I took a good look at his eyes. They were glazed over with pleasure, but it was almost like I could *see* his thoughts. He was thinking about how he never wanted to go another day in his entire life without holding and kissing us.

Our kiss was awesome, if not a little bit hard to concentrate on because I was trying so hard not to come.

"I can't last much longer," Henry whispered into my mouth.

Danny heard what he said and released him. Then he shifted again onto me.

About two seconds after he sucked me into his mouth, though, I blurted out, "Gonna come…." Danny pulled off to watch.

I could also feel Henry's eyes on me, and in a second, I heard, "Shit. Me too." Henry stuck his hand on top of Danny's, and together they finished him off.

IT COULD HAPPEN

Danny knelt for about one second after the show was over, but before he had a chance to blink, we dove onto him.

Henry and I made a good team as we took turns on Danny. I started on his lips while Henry went to town downstairs. After a few minutes, I wanted to taste the rest of him. I touched Henry's shoulder and said, "Switch." Then I watched as Henry dragged his tongue all the way up Danny's skinny body, gave me a deep kiss, and started on Danny's lips.

I bent down so my face was directly above Danny's crotch. He isn't very hairy down there, which at first made him seem sort of young, but his dick was more than ready for further action. My first taste of him was tentative. I hadn't often run the "oral sex on a dude" scenario through my mind. But his reaction to the sensation of my lips on his dick—he sighed and gently smoothed back the hair behind my ear—was so restrained that I felt an urge to make him lose his cool. So I swallowed him down as if I'd done it a hundred times before and tried to recreate all of the tongue motions he'd done on me.

I had no clue if I was doing it right, but he soon pushed my head away and shouted in a panic, "Both of you kiss me—like, now." I knew he wanted all of our mouths together when he let go.

The three of us moaned when our lips came together. Danny moaned with a little more intensity because he was coming, but I could still hear the distinct sound of our three voices at the same time as I felt our lips, wet and a little bruised, but joined together.

Then we climbed under the blankets and snuggled up together.

"Official extended study break," Henry announced and we closed our eyes.

Henry: My life

BRODY PASSES me his cell phone. "Henry, it's your mother."

I've been expecting it, but still I hope I'm ready. "Hey, Mom. It's been a while."

"Your father and I were hoping to get together with you. We stopped by that Daniel Denisco's apartment, but his mother told us you weren't staying there." She clears her voice. "Honestly I was relieved. That building is vile."

"I'm mainly staying with Brody." I resent her remark about Danny's apartment building, but I need to choose my battles wisely if we're to have a conversation. I won't lie. I still hold out some hope that my parents may change their attitude toward my sexuality and my relationship with Danny and Brody. But at the same time, I understand that my hope is probably much closer to fantasy than to reality.

"Yes, that Decker boy." She sighs. "In any event your father and I would like to talk to you about a program suggested by Reverend Wilson that promotes celibacy as an alternative to homosexual behavior. It appears to be a wonderful system that will help you avoid sin."

I guess Mom is aware of the research that suggests gay-conversion therapy is dangerous as well as useless. I looked into it during a rough patch in sophomore year.

But, celibacy?

"No thanks, Mom." I can't hold back a loud sigh. My parents aren't any closer to opening their minds than they were last winter.

"I'm very sorry to hear that," she says and sniffs.

I can hear Dad in the background. "Give me the phone, Lenore. I'll handle this."

"Dad?"

"Yes, Henry. This is your father."

I'm pretty sure I'm ready to face him too, although it's easier since we aren't actually looking at each other. I lean back into the puffy pillows on the big bed, and Brody squeezes my knee, which honestly helps. "Hi."

"We need to discuss graduation. You have relatives who don't know about your change in lifestyle and your departure from the morality with which we raised you. And they expect to attend your graduation."

"They can come to graduation. My cap and gown aren't gonna be rainbow striped." Brody covers his mouth to stifle a fit of laughter, as does Danny, from the couch, where he's designing a cover for the Thomas Bailey Aldrich High School Graduation program.

"Henry, please. We would like your assurance that you will not associate with those two young men at the graduation ceremony. It would embarrass us in front of family members."

I'm glad we're not on speakerphone. Brody and Danny don't need to hear that. "Dad," I say, "Brody Decker and Danny Denisco *are* my family now. I'll be sitting with them during the ceremony, and we'll be going out to lunch with Mr. and Mrs. Decker and Mrs. Denisco after graduation. You guys are welcome to come and same with Grandma and Grandpa and anybody else."

Dad coughs.

"Should I ask the Deckers to increase the number of people on the reservation for the restaurant?" I ask.

He coughs again. I hear Mom in the background, "What did he say, Carter?"

Dad ignores her. "I… well, I suppose I need to consider this." He's quiet for so long I wonder if he hung up. "But, on the outside chance we choose to join you, yes, please ask the Decker family to increase the number by eight."

I smile. "I'll do that. Let me know for sure when you decide."

"Uh… yes, I will."

"I've got to get to graduation practice now."

"Very well. Goodbye, Henry."

I end the call and exhale.

"You blew it," Danny says without looking up from his sketch.

"What the fuck?" I ask. "I think I handled that well."

"I *was* gonna sew rainbow patches on the collar of our gowns. And paint multicolor stripes on our caps. Now I can't."

Brody says, "Too bad. That would have added a lot to the diversity of our graduating class."

We all break into laughter, which we've been doing a lot lately.

At one point not too long ago, I thought I wasn't ever gonna laugh again. But I'm lucky. Plenty of teenagers who get kicked out of

175

their homes for being gay end up on the street. I have two places to live, with people who give a shit.

Free Verse Poetry by Danny D

"It Could Happen"
Someone tells us, "It can't happen."
Voices say, "It can't be done."
"No one does that."
But if it's real, it *can* happen.
Our own story, we can write.
Your *never* isn't real for us.
We'll fly to where it happens.
Three for one, love will be made.
It's our chance to take.

It could happen....

Brody's notebook

THURSDAY, JUNE 4
~~It Could Happen~~
It's Thomas Bailey Aldrich High School Senior Week and we have some time on our hands. And today, free time means inking Henry.
Inking Henry. It sounds like a movie I wouldn't want to miss.

Danny and I went with Henry to the Galleria of Ink, where he got his tattoo. It was hot as hell to watch the tattoo artist work on him, and we got into it. I even got an adrenaline rush by proxy. When we walked out, Henry wore the tattoo of two fingers pointing in opposite directions on his left bicep and the words "I'm With Them."

IT COULD HAPPEN

It was red and raised and sore, but Henry's fine with it because we're a matched trio.

And as far as the other seniors go, for the most part, they see us as Danny, Henry, and Brody—high school sweethearts who've been together forever.

Never thought it could happen.

I guess everybody who writes any kind of book wants to be profound at its conclusion, so a person from a future generation who ends up reading it will take away some meaning. At the same time, I'm aware that there's a fine line between being insightful and being sappy. So I'm not going to write something trite like "you don't know what you have until you lose it." We, in fact, knew what we had, and we lost it for a while anyway. But I started this diary with a feeling that what we wanted we could find together. And I was right.

It's nice to be right. But I had help making it happen. There are three of us writing this story.

And I'd say we're nailing it.

Mia Kerick is the mother of four exceptional children—a daughter in law school, another in dance school, a third studying at Mia's alma mater, Boston College, and her lone son still in high school. She writes LGBTQ romance when not editing National Honor Society essays, offering opinions on college and law school applications, helping to create dance bios, and reviewing English papers. Her husband of twenty-four years has been told by many that he has the patience of Job, but don't ask Mia about this, as it is a sensitive subject.

Mia focuses her stories on emotional growth in turbulent relationships. As she has a great affinity for the tortured hero, there is, at minimum, one in each book. As a teen, Mia filled spiral-bound notebooks with tales of said tortured heroes and stuffed them under her mattress for safekeeping. She is thankful to Dreamspinner Press and Harmony Ink Press for providing alternate places to stash her stories.

Her books have won a Kirkus Recommended Review, a Best YA Lesbian Rainbow Award, a Reader Views' Book by Book Publicity Literary Award, the Jack Eadon Award for Best Book in Contemporary Drama, an Indie Fab Award, and a Royal Dragonfly Award for Cultural Diversity, among other awards.

Mia is a Progressive, a little bit too obsessed by politics, and cheers for each and every victory in the name of human rights. Her only major regret: never having taken typing or computer class in school, destining her to a life consumed with two-fingered pecking and constant prayer to the Gods of Technology.

Contact Mia at miakerick@gmail.com. Visit www.miakerick.com for updates on what is going on in Mia's world, rants, music, parties, and pictures, and maybe even a little bit of inspiration.

ONE VOICE
BOOK TWO

HERE
WITHOUT
YOU

Mia Kerick

One Voice: Book Two

With all of his scratched and dented heart, Nate DeMarco wants to be two places at once, but he's been forced to make an unbearable choice. Having barely survived high school, Nate and his boyfriends, Casey Minton and Zander Zane, are ready to move forward. Casey and Zander have left home to attend Boston City College. Nate remains in New Hampshire to protect his volatile younger sister from their increasingly violent alcoholic uncle. Nate suffers with anger, resentment, and loneliness as what he wants battles against what he feels he must do.

Separated, the young men fight to stay in contact. But they are faced with separate issues. Casey copes with residual fear from having been bullied in high school. Zander obsesses over the establishment of One Voice, the gay-straight alliance at Boston City College. And Nate fights for his sister's survival. Meanwhile, the intensity of the boys' relationship increases, both sexually and emotionally.

Nate's effort to live two lives leads to tragedy, which threatens to blast their relationship apart before they can adjust to the changes in their lives. They must find their way back to a united path before it's too late.

www.dreamspinnerpress.com

OUT OF HIDING

MIA KERICK

After graduating from high school early, twenty-year-old Philippe Bergeron spent the past several years lost among the stars while fishing off the New England coast. A shoulder injury ends his dream of living reclusively on the water, and he finds himself lost among the bright lights of New York City. His older brother, Henri, has asked Philippe to chaperone his seventeen-year-old niece, Sophie, on her tours of the city's legendary dance programs.

Sophie meets with professional dancer and choreographer, Dario Pereira, to prepare a routine for her college auditions. Dario's cool perfection and immaculate style contrast with Philippe's awkward scruffiness, but it wakes desires Philippe thought he'd left behind. When the attraction is surprisingly returned, Dario's confidence won't let Philippe remain invisible. Unsure but curious, Philippe relaxes his rule of isolation, and as the summer progresses, his relationship with Dario leads him to a surprising discovery of his submissive sexual tendencies and a greater sense of self-awareness.

Tragedy threatens to destroy the connections Philippe has made and forces him to retreat into the shadows of his past, far from the radiance of Dario's love. Ultimately, he must decide if it is time to stop hiding and set himself free.

www.dreamspinnerpress.com

A
Package
Deal

MIA KERICK

Robby Dalton is the perfect all-American boy. He played the sports his father chose for him in high school, attended the college his father selected, and has worked hard to conform to his father's macho views. But emotionally he doesn't fit anywhere, and he can't connect with a woman beyond a few uninspired dates. Robby's not in the closet, because he's never guessed he's gay. Now he owns a small commercial construction company, and one night after work he runs into Savannah Meyers. He finds her fascinating and agrees to a date, thinking maybe this woman would be different.

But Savannah has her own agenda. She is looking for a love match for her roommate, Tristan Chartrand, whom she rescued from the streets years ago. He's like a brother, and her only family, so she wants him safe and happy. Her plan seems to begin well, because when Robby meets Tristan, he's surprised to find it's Tristan he wants, not Savannah. But some people in Robby's life don't approve of Tristan's lowly station in life, and some don't approve of Robby being gay. Some people are full of hate and violence, and Robby and Tristan will need courage and strength if a loving future is to be part of the deal.

Life is not as random
as you think.

MIA KERICK
RANDOM
ACTS

Bradley Zelder can't find his way in life. After struggling for nearly a decade, he has yet to complete his college degree. Working as a school custodian, living in blue-collar Landsbury, MA, his love life is as empty as the rest of his existence. But on his way home after another disastrous date, his truck breaks down in upscale Oceanside. When he thinks life can't get any worse, a man who is the epitome of Boston elite and everything Bradley finds attractive and intimidating helps him move his truck to the side of the road. Ashamed of his lot in life, Bradley almost lets the opportunity slip away, but he comes to his senses in time and tracks Caleb down.

From a random act of kindness, romance begins to grow, filling all the dark corners of Bradley's empty life—until a random act of violence threatens to take it all away. Bradley must step up and be the man Caleb believes him to be. Caleb rescued him from a life without hope. Can Bradley rescue him in return?

www.dreamspinnerpress.com

Beggars
and
Choosers

Mia Kerick

After a hard life filled with experiences he'd rather not remember but can't forget, Brett Taylor decides he doesn't need anyone or anything. He gets a job at a bar in a nothing little town where he can fish and race dirt bikes and hide from the world. So naturally as he's walking across the parking lot at his new job, reminding himself how self-reliant he is, he meets someone he can't shove aside.

Brett can't help but admire Cory Butana, the kid who lives above the bar where his father is the principal bartender. Unwanted by either parent, the sweet, personable Cory grew up neglected and hungry for affection. Now he's determined to make something of his life, even if he has to work himself ragged to do it.

Cory shouldn't have to suffer like Brett did, and Brett wants to lend a hand. But when their relationship evolves into something Brett isn't ready to need, he reacts… and the consequences may destroy their fledgling future. With scars like theirs, forgiveness is never easy.

www.dreamspinnerpress.com

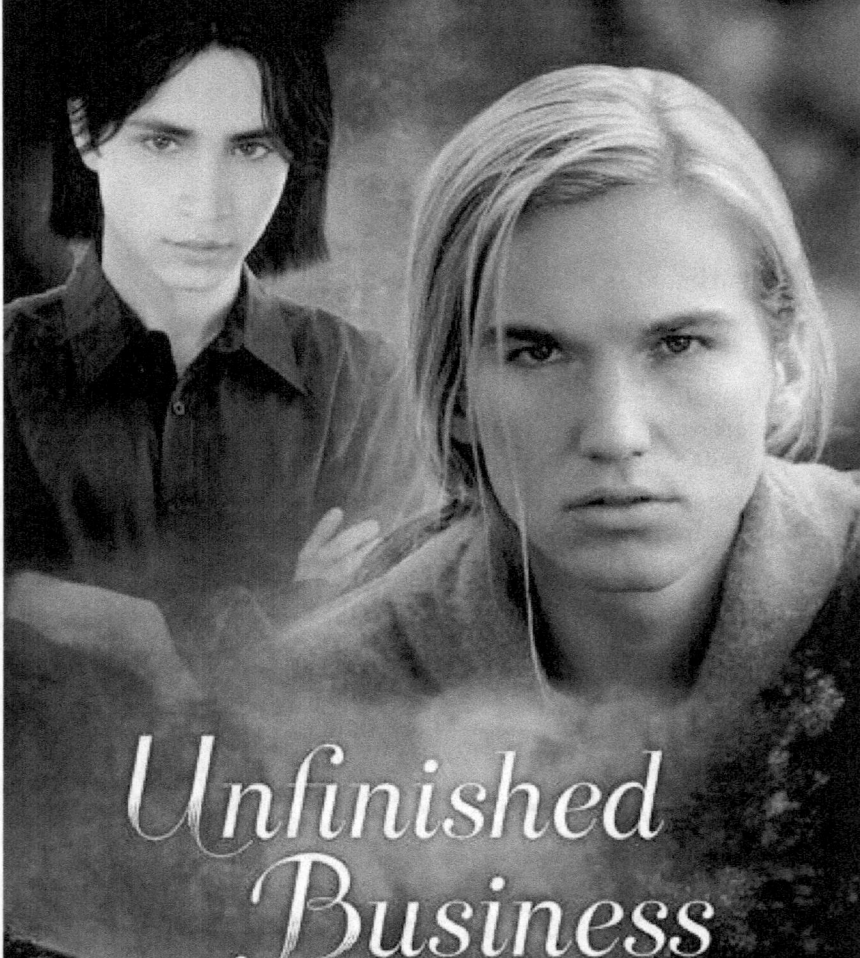

Unfinished Business

Mia Kerick

Sequel to *Beggars and Choosers*

After struggling through dishonesty, betrayal, and the kind of pasts they'd like to leave behind them, Brett Taylor and Cory Butana are back together and starting to build a new life. Brett has a good job. Cory has started college. But not everything goes the way they planned.

Still recovering from the emotional and physical repercussions of a brutal assault, Cory finds himself trapped by his own insecurity and fear, unable to believe that his heart is safe with Brett or that his body is safe without him. On the other hand, Brett has total faith in Cory's love and commitment, even though he still struggles with his own ghosts.

With girls flocking to Brett's side and a wannabe-lover lab partner feeding his doubts, Cory can't find a way to tell Brett about the unfinished business that haunts him. If Brett wants to save him, he'll have to see through Cory's deception in time.

www.dreamspinnerpress.com